D1546250

Mail Order Mystery

Brides of Seattle, Book 1

CYNTHIA WOOLF

Copyright 2017 by Cynthia Woolf

Photo credits – Novel Expressions, Period Images,
Deposit Photos, Romcon Custom Covers

ISBN: 1-947075-34-9
ISBN- 978-1-947075-34-4

DEDICATION

For Jim. Thank you for being my rock, my greatest cheerleader, my husband, my lover and my best friend. You keep me fed, put me to bed when I fall asleep at my desk and take care of me in so many more ways than I've listed here.

I love you, sweetheart!

FOREVER AND A DAY!

ACKNOWLEDGMENTS

For my Just Write partners Michele Callahan, Karen Docter, and Cate Rowan

For my wonderful cover artist, Romcon Custom Covers

For my superb editor, Linda Carroll-Bradd, you make my stories so much better. I don't know what I would do without you.

CHAPTER 1

Seattle, Washington Territory, August 1, 1864

Jason Talbot used his six-foot-six-inch height to look over the heads of the men gathered in the main room of Dolly's Saloon. They were either employed by Pope Mill Company or Talbot Logging, the company Jason and his four brothers founded and had been running for the last ten years.

These were good men, for the most part, some God-fearing, some not. Some drinkers, some not. Most of the lumberjacks had been with Talbot Logging for all of its ten years in business. But now his men wanted wives. They wanted families, and if he couldn't provide the women for them to marry, the men would go elsewhere to work. His wasn't the only logging company in Washington Territory.

In all his thirty-six years he'd never

needed for a plan to come together more than this one. He had to succeed where Asa Mercer had failed. Asa, after promising to return with hundreds of women to Seattle, had come back in mid-May with only ten women. Jason planned on one hundred and his sister would be the catalyst to help him. Suzanne would be able to spread the word as well as place advertisements for the women to come to Seattle. And the icing on the cake was that he, Adam and Drew were going back to bring the women to Seattle, themselves. Jason and his brothers were blessed with pleasing faces, and they had been logging for many years, so their bodies showed their strength. When the women saw them, hopefully, their tall, dark-haired good looks would sell the opportunity to the ladies and entice them to join the venture.

He pounded the gavel on the teak bar in front of him. Dolly Hatfield, the owner, had the beautiful bar shipped in special when she came to town and built the saloon six years ago.

"Quiet. Quiet." Jason yelled over the raised voices of the men in the room.

The two-story building housed the tavern on the main floor and living quarters for Dolly on the upper level.

Dolly wasn't a beautiful woman in the conventional sense. She was blonde and plump with a mole on her left cheek. She had a heart of gold and wouldn't be taken advantage of, but she willingly served as a shoulder for the men to cry on.

Today, Dolly sat on the walkway, upstairs in front of her living quarters, observing the proceedings though not taking part.

"We need women, Jason. We want wives," said Lester Holden, one of Jason's lumberjacks. "All of us."

Jason, as the owner of the lumber company, looked around at the men who filled the room to overflowing. Every chair was taken, and dozens of men stood along the walls, all of them nodding.

"How do you propose that we get women to come here?" asked Alfred Pope, the lumber mill owner.

Pope, who was a good six inches shorter than Jason, was always dressed in a suit like a dandy. Coat, white shirt, silver paisley vest, string tie, and pants. His hair was always parted in the middle and slicked down. Jason had never seen him look any different. He never wore the plaid flannel shirts and wool pants like most of the rest of the men in Seattle, and he certainly never wore buckskins as Jason did either.

"I've been thinking about that," said Jason. "I propose that we import them from Massachusetts. The war has taken most of the men from there, according to my sister, Suzanne, who lives in New Bedford. I'll write today and ask if she can get together women who are looking for husbands and are willing to make the journey. Next week, Clancy will be heading back to New York on his regular run on the *Bonnie Blue*. I want him to pick up the women in addition to our regular supplies."

"Asa Mercer tried that already. What makes you think you can do better?" shouted Mark Delany from the back of the room.

"How many women are you proposing come back here?" asked Craig Rowan, a mill worker. Craig was a hefty, barrel-chested man with blond hair and a beard that hid a double chin.

"One hundred," replied Jason. "And I'll do it even though Asa didn't because I'm me and I have my sister already back there.

She'll send out the notices and have the women sign up before Adam, Drew and I even get there." *I've got two-hundred-and-fifty men who need wives, but I can't bring more than one hundred. The* Bonnie Blue *won't carry more than that.*

"I can't do it," said Clancy Abrams, captain of the *Bonnie Blue*, pulling his pipe from his mouth, his New England accent coloring his words. His captain's hat, which had seen better days, sat on top of his mostly gray hair. Heavy sideburns joined with his gray beard and covered most of his face. "The *Bonnie* won't hold all them women and supplies, too."

"Well," said Jason, running a hand behind his neck. "We'll have you bring the women and whatever supplies you need for the journey with them. After you arrive here and drop off the ladies, you'll return to San Francisco for our regular supplies, even though it's more expensive for us. While we're gone, which will be approximately six months, another ship will be contracted with to bring supplies on a regular basis."

"That I can do," said Clancy.

"How will we know which woman we get?" asked Russell Corbett, a tall, dark-haired lumberjack.

"We won't." Jason knew this arrangement would be a problem. After bouncing the idea off a few of the men, he knew they wanted to just pick a woman and be done with it. "We all have to court the women, and they will decide who they want to marry."

"That is as it should be," said Reverend Peabody, looking over the top of his spectacles. "None of these women will be forced to marry anyone."

"We're payin' one hundred dollars for 'em to git here. They should hafta marry us," said Cy Bailey, a lumberjack known as much for his handlebar mustache as for his prowess with an ax.

"That is not how this will work. We're not buying the women." Jason sighed and ran his hand behind his neck. He knew this would be difficult, but he couldn't believe the idiocy of some of his workers. "We are asking them if they would come with the purpose of marriage in mind, but that is all. If any particular woman doesn't find any of us desirable, so be it. Your money is to cover the expenses of going to Massachusetts and bringing the women back, feeding them on the journey and building them four dormitories to live in when they get here."

He slammed the gavel on the bar.

"That is the way of it, or this venture goes no farther," shouted Jason over the grumbles.

The voices died down.

"Good. Now I'll write my sister and get it on the ship out today. Then Adam, Drew and I will go to Massachusetts to escort, and perhaps help to convince the women to make the journey. By writing Suzanne ahead of our arrival, she can get the ball rolling before we come."

"All right. Okay," said the men. Some shook hands with each other, some good-naturedly cuffed the shoulder of the man next to them, and a few even threw their hats into the air.

"Bar's open," shouted Dolly from the top of the stairs and then she descended to the main floor as graceful as any debutante.

"Thank you for letting us hold our meeting here, Dolly."

"You know I'd do anything for you, Jason," she said with a sultry smile.

"Yes, well, um, thanks again." Jason

walked away toward home wondering what exactly he would say to his sister. He hurried down the steps leading from the saloon to the dirt street. They needed to build boardwalks but hadn't taken the time. They paid for this lack every time the rain came, which in Seattle was often, and turned the street into mud.

He was encouraged by the success of the meeting, but he didn't look forward to the journey. He hadn't been back to New Bedford since Cassie died. Then he'd taken his baby boy and ran, as fast as a ship could take him, from the memories. He'd have to face those painful memories now, and he was not looking forward to that occurance.

Home was a quarter of the way to the top of Bridal Veil Mountain, where he could see people coming by land, but it was Dolly who had a view of the entire harbor from the balcony of her rooms above the saloon. On her balcony, she had a large triangle to let everyone know when the ships were in.

Every ship that docked carried supplies, sometimes mail, and sometimes passengers. Then after they left off their cargo, most filled their holds with lumber—Talbot lumber. Boards for houses, posts for fences

Jason was betting everything on this venture because if he failed he'd lose his lumberjacks. No lumberjacks, no wood for the mill, no business. Room for failure did not exist.

*****

November 4, 1864

Rachel Sawyer sat at her friend Lucy's kitchen table and re-read the advertisement she'd given her. Lucy lived with her parents and wanted to leave that situation as soon as possible, which Rachel understood. Lucy was tired of being under her father's thumb. Lucy's father was not a nice man.

Lucy put her hands around the cup of tea in front of her and listened as Rachel read from the little slip of paper.

Brides wanted. Women willing to travel to Seattle, Washington Territory, are guaranteed husbands of their choosing. Seattle is a logging town with more than three hundred men who want wives. We are looking for one hundred adventurous women to make the journey of a lifetime. Contact Jason Talbot in care of Mrs. Suzanne Pruitt, 2410 Harbor Way, New Bedford, Massachusetts.

"Brides. Wives, Lucy. What do you think?"

She snapped her fingers. "I say sign us up. We sure as heck aren't able to find husbands here. They've all gone to fight the war. Unless, of course, you want to marry old Mr. Keiper. He's always looking for a new wife."

The image of the fat, balding shopkeeper came to mind. Rachel shuddered.

"What's he do with the ones he had? They can't all have met with an accidental end. I believe he kills them so he can get a new one. I should have looked into that. That is a real mystery, but with him, I'm afraid what I might find."

Lucy's shoulders shook and then her head. "I'm signing up for Seattle. You should, too, rather than trying to be a detective concerning Mr. Keiper's missing wives."

Of course, you'd sign up you want to get out of your parent's house, and you love to travel. The idea of faraway places has always drawn you. In a way, I guess I do too. Even though I don't mind living at the boarding house, I want a family of my own. Rachel let out a sigh. "Me, too. I don't want to wait until I'm desperate enough to agree to marry Mr. Keiper."

If only Ezra hadn't gotten himself killed in the war, I wouldn't need to worry about a family. I'd already had one. A family and children. If he'd married me like we planned and then gone to war, I might still have a child of my own. If I continue on the path I'm on I'll never have children.

"Oh, honey. That won't happen."

Rachel looked at her friend. Lucy was Irish, but with raven hair, emerald green eyes and pale skin, she didn't look it. She also didn't have the temper so often associated with red-haired Irish people. Sometimes people called her Black Irish, but she didn't have the dark eyes usually related to someone of Spanish and Irish descent.

"I'm twenty-eight, Lucy. An old maid if there ever was one. I had my chance with Ezra. We were sweethearts for over ten years, ever since we were children. Ezra wanted to wait until he finished medical school and started a practice. Then there was the war and well, he never came home."

Lucy took Rachel's hand in hers. "I know all that and if anyone deserves a family it's you. And you're not an old maid.

You're only two years older than me and I refuse to think of myself as that hideous term. No men are around here to marry. It's not like you turned them down. And Ezra doesn't count. The fool chose the war over you."

Rachel saw the anger that Lucy had every time Rachel mentioned Ezra. Lucy was angrier at Ezra than Rachel was.

"Besides look at you. You're beautiful. Golden blonde hair and big, violet-blue eyes the color of the sky at dusk. If men were around you wouldn't be single."

"I don't know about that. Ezra always said I was rather plain, but he loved me anyway. You on the other hand are beautiful. Let's face it. Neither of us will find men here regardless of our attributes. Eligible men simply don't exist. This ship to Seattle is our last chance for families of our own. I'm signing up, too." She took a deep breath. Excitement roared through her. *Finally, a chance for a husband and family. I'm not passing up this opportunity. I might even find my true love.*

Lucy stood and walked toward the desk in the corner of the kitchen. "It's settled. We'll write the woman and tell her we want to go."

Rachel pounded her hand on the table. "To Hell with writing her. She lives here in New Bedford. I'm going over there first thing tomorrow morning."

Lucy sat then cocked an eyebrow. "Why wait until tomorrow?"

"Because it's too late today. I don't want to be returning home after dark." Rachel didn't like to travel after dark even in a quiet town like New Bedford. It brought back bad memories of another night in a dark hallway in a big house where she'd been a maid and then a bedroom. The man thrusting himself against her, then ripping her dress and shoving her on the bed...NO! She would not think about that night. You'll have to tell your future husband, said a little voice. *No. I don't. He didn't rape me but if his wife hadn't come in when she did... I lost my job and was never so glad to be unemployed. I went to the factory after that. The position didn't pay as much and I had to move back to the boarding house, but at least I was safe.* Her hands gripped the table so tight her knuckles were white. She relaxed and let go of the table letting her hands fall into her lap.

"I'll go with you tomorrow. We can share a Hansom cab there and back."

"It's a deal. See you in the morning at nine o'clock."

*****

Lucy was at the boarding house right on time. She'd come in a Hansom cab.

Rachel didn't even invite her in but took off toward the taxi waiting out front.

"Let's go."

Rachel grabbed Lucy's arm and they hurried to the cab. Rachel would contact her parents after all the arrangements were made so there was no backing down.

Ten minutes later they stood in front of Suzanne Pruitt's home.

Rachel swallowed hard. "Are you ready?"

Lucy nodded. "Terrified, but ready."

They walked to the front door, and Rachel knocked firmly.

A middle-aged woman with gray hair and a white cap opened the door.

"May I help you, young ladies?"

"Yes, we're here about...um..."

"You're here about the ad are you not?"

"Yes, ma'am, we are." Rachel twisted the strings of her reticule in her hands.

"Follow me, ladies."

She led them to what Rachel saw was the parlor. A half dozen women were already gathered.

"Are you all here about the ad?" Rachel asked the woman closest to her, a vibrant redhead. At the same time, she wondered why more women hadn't shown up. Maybe the early hour had put them off and they would be coming later. She made a point of memorizing everything she could about the women in the room. After all, a good detective is always observant of their environment.

"Yes. What about you?" asked the woman with the dark auburn hair.

"Yes. We saw the ad yesterday. I'm Rachel Sawyer and this is my friend Lucy Davison."

"We did, too. I'm Nicole Wescott." She turned to the other ladies in the room. "That is Karen Martell with the red hair, Bethany Van Ness, in the blue dress, Charlene Belcher, in the pink dress, Bertha Corrigan, with the blonde hair, and Nancy Picozzi in the green dress."

"Pleased to meet all you ladies," said Rachel and Lucy together. They turned to each other and laughed.

"I'm a little nervous," admitted Rachel. This was the strangest room she'd ever seen. Every bit of wall space was taken up with bookshelves…full bookshelves. She loved the idea but where would she get that many books. A reading area with a sofa and two chairs was in front of the fireplace. She liked everything about the room and would love to have one like it in her new home.

"We all are," said Nicole. "But we all hope the roster isn't full and they will take us all."

"Good morning, ladies," said a pretty blonde, and very pregnant, woman. "I'm Suzanne Pruitt, and you ladies are here to sign up for the trip to Seattle with my brothers. They are not here yet, won't be for another week or so, but we are getting the ball rolling by signing up ladies now."

"Will they be able to take us all?" asked Lucy.

"Oh, yes. My brothers are hoping to get one hundred women, and you all are the first to sign up."

Suzanne walked over to the small table next to Rachel, which she would swear was put in the room just for the purpose of signing up the women. The piece of furniture didn't match anything else in the room.

"Now, ladies," Suzanne clapped her hands to get their attention. "Please line up. Everyone is requested to sign the roster. Include your names and addresses, please. My brothers are anticipated to arrive between the twelfth and the fourteenth of this month. I've requested the hall at the *Presbeterian* church around the corner for them to meet and greet everyone. Please plan on being there on the fifteenth so my brothers can meet you and you can ask any questions that you may have."

All eight of the women lined up and in an orderly fashion signed their names to the list. Rachel was the first, Lucy the second because of their proximity to the table. After Lucy finished signing, Rachel took her by the arm and grinned.

"We did it. We signed up to be mail-order brides. Can you believe it, Luce? We'll be married probably within the year. Aren't you excited?"

"Yes, I want to yell out my excitement, but that wouldn't be ladylike."

Rachel laughed. "No, I guess it

wouldn't."

"Very good. Now the next meeting will be at the Presbyterian church on the corner of Midway and Cape Cod Avenues on November 15th. In the meantime, ladies, get your affairs in order so you'll be ready to leave with little notice," said Suzanne.

"This is happening," whispered Lucy to Rachel.

Rachel nodded. "Yes. It really is. We'll finally have our own families.

"Oh, and ladies," said Suzanne. "No more than one trunk each and make sure your name is clearly marked on the trunk. Space on the ship will be at a premium. The trunks will be in the hold and difficult to reach. I recommend that you do not take your hoops but bring dresses without them. Shorten the hems of your skirts as needed. None of the women already in Seattle wear hoops, as they would hamper their ability to do their chores and get around. This is a unlike any you've ever know. Seattle is very small. Trust me when I say you'll be in an entirely different world."

CHAPTER 2

November 14, 1864
Home of Suzanne and Arthur Pruitt

Jason knocked on the front door of Suzanne Pruitt's home. He, Adam and Drew waited on the porch to be admitted each of them wearing a sheepskin coat for protection against the freezing weather. Hopefully, Suzanne had placed the ads in the papers and started a roster of the ladies who wanted to sign up to be mail-order brides.

The door opened, and their pretty blonde, blue-eyed sister stood there, heavily pregnant and radiant.

"Jason!"

She threw herself into Jason's arms.

He caught her as he'd done since she was a baby. Suzanne was the youngest of the Talbot children, just twenty-six and expecting her fourth child. She'd married young, at least as far as Jason was concerned, at seventeen but she had been determined to marry Arthur Pruitt and told Jason so.

What his beautiful sister saw in the mild-mannered, brown-haired, bespectacled, Arthur Pruitt, he couldn't fathom, but he realized there was nothing he could say to change her mind and so he'd agreed. They married just before Jason and his brothers all left for Seattle and Bridal Veil Mountain, the mountain of timber they'd bought sight unseen. That was almost ten years ago now, just after Jason's wife Cassie died while birthing Billy. The pain the memory brought had lessened over the years, but his stomach still clenched when he thought of it. His chest didn't ache anymore though, and for that he was grateful. Just ten days after her death, he'd taken his baby son with him and raised him on that mountain.

"Come in, quickly. Get out of the cold."

She stood back and let them pass.

Standing in the foyer was Suzanne's husband and their three children, Gillian, age nine, Scott, age six and Peter, age three. Arthur's hair was graying, but his eyes twinkled as he observed his wife. Jason could only imagine that happiness is what gave his eyes the twinkle.

Gillian was the image of her mother right down to the blonde hair and blue eyes. Whereas Scott and Peter resembled their father, with brown hair but Scott also had his mother's blue eyes, while Peter's were brown.

Billy would have loved to meet his cousins. Jason wished he'd brought the boy along.

"Gillian." Her mother pointed at the brothers. "You and Scott take their coats and put them on the sofa in Daddy's den."

"Yes, Mama." She went to Jason. "May I take your coat please, Uncle Jason?"

Jason shrugged out of his coat. "Here you go, sweet girl."

Adam and Drew each took off their coats and gave them to the children. Peter tried to pick up Drew's jacket, but he was too little, and the coat dragged along the floor.

Drew chuckled.

Suzanne didn't. She took the coat from Peter. "Baby, you're not big enough to take this yet. Let Gillian get this for you."

Peter hung his head. "Yes, Mama."

Suzanne bent over and kissed her baby's head. "Next year, you'll be big enough, okay?"

He nodded and ran after the other two children.

Jason walked forward, arm outstretched.

"Arthur. Good to see you."

He shook Jason's hand.

"And you Jason."

Jason was the tallest brother. Adam, with his golden hair and blue eyes, stood a couple of inches taller than Drew, who was the shortest of the five brothers at five feet, ten inches. Like Jason, he had dark brown hair and green eyes. Each of the brothers hugged their sister, then came forward to shake hands with their brother-in-law.

Jason looked around the foyer. It was two stories tall with windows on both sides of the door letting in plenty of light. The floor was oak, polished to a high sheen and covered for the most part with an Oriental rug.

"You have a beautiful home."

"Thank you. Come with me." Suzanne turned and walked down the hall covered in dark green carpet with a paisley design woven in silver down the middle. The walls were painted pale green with darker accents above the chair rail and cream-colored wallpaper with vines and roses below. The air in the room seemed suddenly chilly from a breeze blowing through an open window. Suzanne closed the window and then took them to the parlor where a roaring fire burned.

In the parlor the walls of the room were covered in bookshelves. Jason remembered how much Suzanne had always loved to read and from the time she was old enough to read on her own, she'd said she would have a room that had nothing but bookshelves on the walls. The wall across from the door was all windows above a window seat that looked out over the backyard garden. He wished he had room for a library like this at home. Billy would love it. He took after his aunt in that respect…he loved to read.

A blue brocade sofa and matching solid blue over-stuffed chairs formed a semi-circle in front of the fireplace.

Tables with lamps on them sat between the chairs and the sofa, so light to read by was in ample supply.

Arthur and Suzanne's home was so different from the one in which Jason and his brothers occupied. They didn't have any of the elaborate furniture or wallpaper. Their home was natural wood, inside and out. A log home held together with mud between the logs to keep out the weather. Practical not fancy.

"I love your home. There are many aspects, I'd like to do to our home, but we live rather rustically," said Adam.

"Thank you," said Arthur. "When Suzie saw this room she was sold on the house and had to have it." He pulled a cord on the wall. "The rest of the house could have been derelict, and she wouldn't have cared."

Suzanne and Arthur sat on the sofa with Jason. Drew and Adam sat in the two chairs.

Shortly after that, a stout woman, of indeterminate age, with a white cap atop her steel-gray hair, wearing a black dress with white collar and cuffs, appeared.

"You rang, sir?"

"Yes, Mrs. Gates would you bring us a tea tray and some sandwiches, please? I daresay my brothers-in-law are starving," said Arthur.

"Right away." She ducked her chin and left.

Jason pointed after the woman who was the housekeeper. "Mrs. Gates is new. What happened to Mrs. Caldwell?"

"She retired. Went to live with her sister in the country," said Suzanne. "Mrs. Gates has been with us for six years now. Since just after Scott was born. If you'd come back to visit you'd have known."

Jason ran his hand behind his neck. "You know we couldn't take that much time off from the business. We've all been busy getting it running profitably, but now that it is, we'll visit more often."

"Now that we've caught up let's get down to business." Drew sat in one of the chairs, leaned forward and rested a hand on his knee while waving the other in front of him for their attention.

Suzanne shook her head and rolled her eyes.

"That's just like you Drew, so anxious to get on with everything. You need to take life slower and see what's happening around you. Maybe when you find your bride, you'll settle down."

Drew shook his head and put his hands up in front of him.

"Oh, no. None of these women is for me. I'm not ready to get married. May never be. I'm not letting any woman tie me down."

Suzanne laughed.

"We'll see. I bet that out of these women if you actually get one hundred to sign on, each of you will find a bride."

All of the brothers shook their heads.

"These women are not for us," insisted Jason. "They are for our men. Our lumberjacks and mill workers. Our bartenders and shopkeepers."

"But none are for you, is that right?" Suzanne scowled.

Her tone was full of sarcasm, but Jason ignored it. "That's right."

"You will be with these women for three months on that ship, and you don't' think the possibility exists that you'll fall in love and want to marry one?"

"No, I don't," said Jason sadly remembering his marriage to Cassie. "I've been married. I had my shot."

"Perhaps," said Suzanne. "But maybe you'll have another."

She reached over and placed her hand on her brother's knee. "You're thirty-six, Jason. Cassie never meant for you to be alone forever."

He didn't answer. His throat was suddenly dry, and his chest tightened as he remembered his loss. Staring out the window, he knew what he'd had with Cassie was special, and he was not likely to find that kind of love again. They'd had the same interests, same likes, and dislikes. They'd married young. He was nineteen and she was just seventeen. In the seven years they were married, they never fought. Some people would have called their marriage boring. He called it comfortable.

He turned back and peered at his sister. "Did you place the advertisements?"

Suzanne nodded. "In papers here in New Bedford, as well as in Boston, and New York."

"Good. Have you had any responses?"

Suzanne smiled.

"Yes, I've already signed up quite a few and more are interested and are *thinking* about it. These women want husbands, but the thought of leaving family and friends for a wild land on the other side of the country is daunting, to say the least."

"Is there someplace we can interview these women and make sure they are suitable wives for our men?" asked Adam.

"Yes," said Drew. "We don't want prostitutes or sickly women. They need to be hardy not only for the journey but for the reality of life when we reach Seattle. It's not like living in Massachusetts where you can go to a store and buy just about anything. They'll have to make a lot of things—butter, bread, jams, and clothes if they want them faster than in a couple of months."

"I have reserved the Presbyterian church for tomorrow for the interviews. How long are you planning on staying?" asked Suzanne as she glanced at her brothers.

Jason went to the fireplace and rubbed his cold hands in front of the inferno blazing in the fire box. "No longer than two months. If we don't have one hundred brides by the end of January, we'll sail anyway. By that time the ocean has settled some and sailing will be easier. If more women show up after we leave, then you can send them to the next ship to Seattle. Tell the captain that Jason Talbot will pay him for their passage. If we get one hundred in the first month, we'll set sail sooner than anticipated."

The door opened, and Mrs. Gates entered pushing a tea cart.

"Oh, good here are the refreshments. Thank you, Mrs. Gates. You can leave the cart right there by the chair." Suzanne turned to them and waved a hand toward the food. "Gentlemen, you're fully capable of serving yourselves. Arthur, love, would you bring me a cup of tea and two cucumber sandwiches, please?"

"Of course, my dear."

"See that's another reason not to get married…all those my love and my dears," Drew shuttered.

Arthur chuckled. He shook his graying head. Jason had no doubt he'd received every gray hair from living with Suzanne. She could be a trial to live with, yet Arthur smiled as he gazed at her, then picked up her hand and kissed the top. He was always doing a little something like that, acting as though they were still courting. Was that why Suzanne seemed so happy?

Did I ever look at Cassie like that? I loved her, but ours was a different kind of marriage. We were reserved. Even making love was a quiet thing with us. I can't remember her ever once calling my name at orgasm or any name for that matter. With her, it was more of a shudder, and she was done. If I was to marry again, I hope I find someone with passion, screaming-my-name-

in-ecstasy kind of passion.

Jason smiled at his wayward thoughts. Nothing would come of it anyway. He was not in the market for a new wife.

*****

November 15, 1864
Presbyterian Church, New Bedford, Massachusetts

"Ladies. Ladies, please, take your seats."

The man shouted over the din of whispered voices.

The voices died down, all gazes riveted toward the handsome man in front. "Ladies, everyone will get a berth on the ship, but I need to know who you all are for the captain's manifest. My name is Jason Talbot and my brothers, Adam and Drew," he pointed at the two extraordinarily handsome men behind him. "We are here to find one hundred ladies to travel to Seattle, Washington Territory, to become wives to our lumberjacks and the other workers in the town. Now, I'll read the names on this list, and please respond with an "Aye" if your name is called. Rachel Sawyer."

"Aye," said Rachel.

"Lucy Davison," called Jason.

"Aye," said Lucy.

Rachel tried to keep her mind concentrating on everyone's appearance, practicing her detecting skills, but instead, every bit of her attention was on the man at the front of the room. Jason Talbot. She didn't think she'd ever seen a more handsome, mature man. Tall, with wide shoulders, a trim waist, and long legs, he was the picture of every man she'd ever dreamed of. His hair was sable brown with just a couple of pale sun-streaks and curled on the ends, framing his face and spilling over his collar. Golden brown skin, probably from working outdoors, made his teeth seem even whiter when he smiled, and currently, he smiled at her, his sky-blue eyes twinkling as though he knew something special.

Rachel stood, unknowing of what was happening around her.

"Miss Sawyer? Do you have a question?" he asked her.

"Huh. Oh, no, no thank you. I'm fine." She felt herself blush and glanced away.

Lucy giggled and pulled Rachel away. As they hurried to the back of the room, Rachel saw that the church sanctuary they were in had pews enough to hold about 150 people. Now space was filled by ladies of all shapes and sizes from absolutely skinny to fat and everywhere in-between. Their ages ran the gamut from eighteen to past forty.

"Rachel. What's the matter with you?" Lucy's brows were lowered, and she wasn't giggling anymore. "I've never seen you respond to a man like that. You were…mesmerized for lack of a better word."

Embarrassed, she snapped, "I wasn't."

"You were."

Rachel's shoulders sagged, and she closed her eyes frowning. "Oh, dear, did I make a fool of myself?"

"Not really and he didn't smile at anyone else like he did you."

"Really?" Rachel sat up straight and dared a glance to the front. He was still looking her way. She quickly lowered her gaze.

"Yes, really. You've never done the curls before. I like it." She jutted her chin toward Rachel. "They draw the emphasis to your violet-blue eyes."

"Ah, Lucy, you're so sweet. What would I do without you? I was afraid I hadn't done the curls correctly. I probably shouldn't have done them, since I won't be wearing curls in my hair on a regular basis but I wanted to look especially nice. I'm glad you like my appearance, I hope he does, too." She rolled her gaze toward the front of the room and Jason Talbot.

"You won't have to find out, I will, because I'm going to Seattle, too."

Rachel squeezed Lucy's hand.

"And I'm so glad you are."

They worked their way back to the front of the pews with the other women who had been checked off the list and approved Rachel guessed, although she hadn't seen a woman yet who was refused. She and Lucy sat in the cushioned pew and waited for whatever was to happen next.

Standing at the podium addressing all the ladies assembled was another brother.

"Hi, ladies. I'm Adam Talbot. It's my job to explain to you what will happen when we leave here. From the looks of this turnout, we'll be leaving in about a month. That period should give you time to settle your affairs and be ready to leave on December 15th. Is anyone present who cannot make that deadline?"

At first, no one moved, then a single hand was tentatively lifted. The woman was striking with black hair, pale skin, dark blue eyes and a firm jut to her chin.

"Yes, miss, what is your question?"

"My son will not be out of school by that time. They don't get out until the 20th."

"A son?" repeated Adam.

Rachel leaned over and whispered to Lucy. "I wouldn't want to bring a child on this trip. I think it would be too difficult.

"Yes," said the woman. "You didn't say that we couldn't have children, only that we were not currently married to anyone. Well, I'm not married and I have two children."

"Well, I don't know, I…uh, Jason," said Adam, looking over his shoulder to where Jason sat with Drew and Suzanne.

"Yes?" asked Jason.

"This lady has children."

The woman now looked at Jason. "That's right I do, Mr. Talbot, two of them. Before you say I can't go, you should know that I'm a qualified midwife and almost a doctor." She turned her head and glanced at the audience of women. "I didn't quite finish my college education because I got married, but you'll need me, Mr. Talbot. When these ladies get married, babies are the next to come."

"Well, Miss—"

"It's Mrs. Martell, Karen Martell."

"Well, Mrs. Martell, you're quite right we will need your services and not just as a midwife. We don't have a doctor in Seattle, your knowledge in that area would be quite useful as well, so I suggest that you withdraw your children a little early from school."

"There's only one child that's in school, my son, Larry. He's in first grade."

Jason cocked his head to one side and narrowed his eyes. "At such a young age, leaving school five days early will not hurt him, and you know that. What is really your problem, Mrs. Martell?"

Rachel couldn't imagine bringing children on this trip, which would be hard enough for the adults, much more so on the children.

Karen Martell squared her shoulders and raised her chin. "I wanted to know what you would say about children coming. There are many widows with children who are seeking new husbands."

"With a few exceptions, we prefer

women without children. We can't guarantee that women with children will find husbands. Many men do not want a ready-made family," said Adam Talbot. "Others won't mind at all, but we can't say which will and which won't."

Karen nodded. "I understand."

She got up and started to leave.

"Mrs. Martell, exceptions will always be made, and you are an exception. We'd like for you to accompany us to Seattle," said Adam, smiling. "Your selection of men agreeable to marriage may be smaller due to your offspring."

Rachel observed Karen Martell as a smile crossed her face. She looked absolutely radiant.

"Thank you. We'll be ready on the 15th," said Mrs. Martell.

"Good," said Adam. "Very good."

Rachel watched Adam Talbot as he stared at the Martell woman and spotted definite interest on his part. Karen Martell seemed to be oblivious or was purposely ignoring him.

She didn't know why she was watching them when Jason Talbot was who interested her.

*****

Rachel wrote her mother to let her know what was happening in her life. Pennsylvania was too far away to go for a visit before she left.

December 1, 1864

Dear Mama,

I'm leaving New Bedford for Seattle in the Washington Territory. It is very far away, clear on the other side of the continent, north of California. I've decided to become a mail-order bride. We lost so many young men in this war, there is no one left here to marry. Sometimes I wish Ezra to Hades for bringing me here and then deciding to join the Army and get himself killed.

He promised that wouldn't happen that doctors are safe, but they weren't, and he died. You already know this, I know, but I want you to understand why I'm doing what I am.

One of the men who came here to take brides back to Seattle and his lumberjacks is named Jason Talbot. I felt like I was hit by a lightning bolt when I saw him. I'm doing something I've never done before and going after the man I want.

I waited for Ezra, and we ended up engaged for almost ten years because he had to finish school and then establish a practice. But then the war came, and he said he needed to do his part. I won't let that happen again.

Wish me well, Mama. I'll write again from Seattle.

I love you so much. Kiss Daddy for me.
Always your daughter,
Rachel

*****

December 15, 1864
Docks at New Bedford, Massachusetts

Jason stood on the bridge of the ship and watched his goal of one hundred women come on board the *Bonnie Blue*. Space being at a premium, he, Adam, and Drew shared the captain's quarters with Clancy. Just the thought of that made him tired. It was going to be a long journey.

That didn't matter. What did matter was they'd achieved their goal. One hundred women…one hundred brides. Ninety-nine, if Adam had his way. Jason saw that Adam hadn't been able to get his gaze off of Karen

Martell since meeting her that first day.

Jason had to admit she was a striking-looking woman, but his tastes went to the more understated. He thought that Rachel Sawyer was about the prettiest little thing he'd seen in a long while. If he'd been looking for a bride, she would be the one he'd set his sights on, but he wasn't looking. He had Billy, and he'd had his love with Cassie. That was enough. But that realization didn't stop him from looking at the ravishing Miss Sawyer. Or from being lonely at night when all was still.

He wondered if he should worry about Billy with his uncles, but they'd raised him as much as Adam had. When Billy was a baby each one of his brothers volunteered for baby duty so Adam didn't have to do the job alone. They'd each fed him, changed his diapers, bathed him and gotten up in the middle of the night with him. Billy was one lucky boy. The situation was almost like he had five fathers. Was that enough? Did he need a mother?

Jason searched the faces of the women and found Rachel. She was in close conversation with her friend...Lucy. Now she was a funny woman. Clumsy to a fault…at least when Drew was around. Jason wondered if Drew knew one the of the brides was interested in him.

The loading of the ship took most of the morning, but they finally had everyone on board, and the boat was ready to set sail on tomorrow morning's tide. Jason fully expected to have brides who changed their mind before they left port. He sincerely hoped Miss Sawyer wasn't among them.

The *Bonnie Blue* set sail on the morning tide. By the time most of the brides awoke they would be way out to sea and not able to see land much less go back. There was no turning back. Only forward.

*****

Meals were eaten in shifts. There was enough room in the mess to accommodate twenty-five at a time. After everyone had eaten, she decided to approach him. Rachel watched Jason Talbot for weeks before finally getting the courage to speak to him. As they sailed south along the coast of South America, she decided it was now or never.

"Mr. Talbot."

"Yes, Miss Sawyer. How can I assist you?"

"I know I'm being terribly forward," she

felt herself blush. She couldn't control the reaction even when she wanted to. "But I wondered if you, um, knew anything about astronomy. The stars seem especially bright tonight."

He smiled. "I do know a little bit about the sky, would you care to join me on deck and I'll tell you what little I know."

She headed up to the deck, and he followed because the narrow passageways were barely wider than one person.

And so it began.

*****

Rachel waited by the rail, staring out into the calm, blue ocean. She was sure Jason would be there soon, even though she hadn't asked him to come again, she knew he watched her leave the ship's mess. They ate at the same time, though not at the same table.

He sat with his brothers, the captain and the first mate.

She sat with Lucy and several of the other women, including Karen Martell and her two children, six-year-old Larry and three-year-old Patty. The children were very well behaved considering the confinement of the ship, but Karen kept them occupied with games and projects. She never let either of them go topside without her and another bride. The deck was just too dangerous.

Even though most of the brides turned out to be good sailors, there were a few who simply could not go topside, for the vastness of the sea around them made them ill.

Those that did go outside learned to sway with the rolling of the ship over the ocean waves. Most very easily and quickly.

Rachel was one of those. She loved the ocean. The smell of the sea after a storm was amazing. She'd sneaked up to the deck during their first storm and had been mesmerized by the lightning striking in the distance.

She found out later that what she'd done was very dangerous. Lightning and wooden ships do not mix. It was not uncommon for the lightning to strike the main mast of a ship, causing it to shiver or long splinters to be blown from it, occasionally injuring a sailor or knocking him off the deck, which ·in a stormy ocean usually meant death. The sails also sometimes caught fire, but the captain and crew smothered the fire with the help of the rain and wind.

Knowing those things did not stop her

from going up to the deck to watch the storm from the top stair before actually going on the deck. Jason knew he could find her there and she often was just waiting for him so they could spend time together.

One night she watched Jason stand behind Clancy who was at the wheel. Jason had his hands on his hips, and the wind blew through his hair making it curl all over. He stood there like the world was his for the taking. To her, he looked magnificent.

They only met at night which made her sad, but she would rather have him some of the time than not at all. He wasn't ready, maybe never would be ready, to meet her during the day when his brothers might see.

She didn't blame him. Rachel was the same way with Lucy. She didn't want to hear her lectures about falling too soon for a man who is obviously unavailable.

"Jason, why won't you meet me during the day? Are you ashamed of me?"

He closed his eyes and put his arms around her.

"No, I'm not ashamed of you. Never. You are the kindest, smartest and most beautiful woman I know, but I'm not a free man."

She pulled away and turned her back to him. "You're married?"

Jason placed an arm around her shoulders and tugged her back against his chest. "I was. Cassie died birthing our son, Billy. He's nearly ten now."

"If your wife died ten years ago, how does that make you not a free man?"

"I loved Cassie. I still do. I wouldn't be able to give you what you need."

Rachel turned in his arms, put hers around his waist and glared up at him. "You don't know what I need. You are what I need...for now. So just kiss me, Jason, and let me make my own decisions."

She was grasping for whatever happiness she could get. Even if her contentment was fleeting and would end soon, Rachel would take it and try like Hell to figure out a way to make him understand that he could care for her, too.

Lord, how do you fight a ghost?

CHAPTER 3

April 21, 1865
The last night on the Bonnie Blue, before reaching Seattle

After more than three months at sea, Jason still watched her in the moonlight. Her golden hair shimmered silver under the full moon.

"You shouldn't lean against that rail, Miss Sawyer."

"Why not Mr. Talbot?"

She continued to look out over the ocean, seemingly undisturbed by his presence.

"It might give way even under your slight weight."

She laughed, a rich, throaty sound. "Don't be ridiculous, Mr. Talbot. I've watched the sailors walking along the rail numerous times for sport. What's the *real* reason you don't want me to stand here?"

He didn't move but spoke from out of the dark.

"I was hoping you'd join me here in the shadow of the main mast. It's a beautiful night."

She turned and reached him before he'd spoken his last word.

He reached out and pushed an errant lock of hair behind her ear but the slight breeze brought the tress out again. She wore her hair loose. Golden waves cascading down her back. Jason wanted to reach out and grab a handful and pull her close.

She must have been reading his mind for she sidled up next to him.

"Now that I'm here what do you propose to do with me?"

"This."

He lowered his head and took her lips with his in a searing kiss. He ravaged her mouth.

She wrapped her arms around his neck.

Jason pulled her close, close enough that couldn't he hide his readiness for her.

Finally, he broke the kiss but continued to hold her.

"You do tempt me, Rachel, like I haven't been in a very long time."

She ran her fingertip through the curls at his collar without letting him go. "I'm glad

I'm not the only one who feels this way."

He leaned down and whispered in her ear. "I could easily take you…"

She breathed the words back to him. "And I could let you…"

He raised his head and shook it lightly. "But you won't."

She leaned her head to the right and sighed. "And you won't."

He ran his hand through her silky hair as he'd wanted to and then when the breeze took the curls from his hand he snatched the tresses back.

"Where does that leave us?" He brought the silken strands to his nose and smelled her rose soap.

"Where we started when this trip began, three months ago. Too far apart. And now that the voyage has nearly ended, we are still too far apart. I want a chance to prove my love for you, but you don't want my love," she dipped her chin. "So here we are, playing our last midnight game."

"Yes, tomorrow we sail into Seattle."

"Kiss me, Jason. Kiss me so I remember it forever."

He drew her into his arms, lowered his head, sipped at her lips, gently, then more forcefully until they melded together so close that where he stopped and she began he couldn't tell.

Jason pulled back first.

"I must stop before I do take you right here on the deck like some cheap doxie."

"I wouldn't stop you."

"I know. That's why I must stop. Reality intrudes, as always." *Rachel is so brazen in her attitude, but if she hadn't been, we would never have had the time we did. She's so different than Cassie, but I like that. But I must stop. We have no future, and I can't pretend any longer.*

He released her, his hands lingering on her shoulders before dropping to his sides.

"Good night, Miss Sawyer."

She looked up at him, and in the moonlight, he saw the tears in her eyes, but she didn't let them fall.

Instead, she pulled her coat tighter and her scarf higher on her neck, covering the pretty purple silk dress she wore. Did Rachel know it was his favorite? Did she wear it for him tonight? He hoped so.

"Good night, Mr. Talbot."

Did he want her or not? He watched as she turned away and walked across the deck, head held high, to the stairs going below.

Jason stood there for a long time, easily swaying with the ship as she sailed over the water, letting his body relax. Letting his mind release her and wishing his heart could let go of her as quickly. Did he love her? No. He couldn't. He still loved Cassie. And that was that. Wasn't it?

Just before dawn, he returned to the room he shared with his brothers and Clancy. Back to life as he knew it. Away from the siren's song that Rachel wove around him without even trying. Lord, if she knew what she was doing he'd be lost, unable to resist her call to him, to his body.

*****

April 22, 1865
Seattle, Washington Territory

Rachel heard the clang of a metal triangle and saw a blonde woman on the balcony of a two-story building running the metal rod around and around the inside of the triangle.

"Boat's in. The boat is in," she shouted loud enough for Rachel to barely hear the words.

On the street below the woman, people stopped what they were doing, and Rachel watched as lines of people headed down to the dock.

Michael and Gabe Talbot were the first off the ship and helped the sailors tie off the *Bonnie Blue*.

Drew was the next off the ship. When he reached the dock, he had a little trouble walking, needing to get his 'land' legs after three months at sea.

Everyone on the boat was like that except Clancy. He had the same swagger on land and sea.

Clancy made his way toward the two-story building, leaving the Talbots to deal with the brides.

Jason had told her that four dormitories were being built with bathing rooms and a water pump in the kitchen and the bathing room. Each bathing room had a pot-bellied stove to heat the room and the water. There was a metal bucket for heating the water on the stove.

He said each kitchen had a four burner stove, dishes, pots and pans, cutlery and a pantry full of all kinds of food stuffs. The pump supplied the water to the sink. The tables in each kitchen easily sat twelve and fourteen could be squeezed in if needed on the long benches setting on either side. A captain's chair sat on either end. The ice boxes were supposed to be packed with meat, milk, and butter. The brides would not starve while living in Seattle.

As she came down the gangplank, Rachel looked over the tiny town and wondered what in the world she'd gotten herself into. Compared to New Bedford, Seattle was a shanty town though she would never tell Jason that.

The town was surrounded by tall pine trees, and a tall mountain with snow on top rose in the distance. She had to admit the surrounding area was beautiful in a wild sort of way.

When the women were off the ship, they all started asking questions of Rachel. She had been chosen the leader of the brides, probably because of her perceived relationship with Jason.

"Ladies. Please." She waved her arms up and down in front of her. "We'll have a meeting here in Dormitory One. Tonight at seven. In the meantime, the sailors will deliver your trunks. I hope that each of you put your name on them as requested, so you can be found." *I put my gun in the bottom of my trunk. I hope they don't deliver it to someone else. I might need that weapon out here in the wilderness.*

From where she stood on the porch of building one, she broke the women into groups of twenty-five and appointed a dormitory leader for each building. She was the leader in building one, Karen Martell was the leader of dormitory two, Nicole Wescott was the leader in building three and Charlene "Charli" Belcher held the position in building four.

The heads of the 'houses' as they were called had an actual bedroom, whereas the rest of the women had a cot and a small closet about twelve inches wide and eighteen inches deep, as well as three pegs on the wall. Their trunks would set at the foot of the bed. Privacy was hard to come by in the buildings except in the bathing rooms. Each bed stood only about three to four feet from the next one in the line and two lines of twelve beds, one along each wall.

Outside the dormitories, Rachel directed the sailors with the ladies trunks, to the building each woman was in.

"So, what do you think?" asked Jason from behind her.

Rachel jumped and turned to face him.

"You startled me. I didn't know you were behind me."

"I'm sorry. I didn't mean to frighten you." He lowered his voice to a whisper. "If we were alone, I'd show you my real intent."

Rachel's blood pounded in her veins at the thought of being alone with Jason Talbot in a building with twenty-five beds.

He softly chuckled.

"I see your thoughts are similar to my own."

"Stop that. I'll be red until tomorrow if you don't quit with your sinful thoughts and suggestions." But then she wondered what was going on. Just last night he'd wanted to end their liaison.

"I didn't make any suggestions. Those are your minds inclinations. The fact that my mind is inclined the same way is neither here nor there."

He smiled and she knew he was correct. Rachel did have those thoughts. But only with Jason. Since her assault, he was the first man she'd gotten close to. Now she was confused. What did he want?

"Well, I never," she huffed, moved away from him to the bottom of the steps leading to building one and then turned to stare at him.

He grinned. "That's obvious."

Rachel raised her eyes toward heaven and then shook her head.

"You're impossible."

"No." He suddenly sighed and lowered his gaze to the ground. "We are impossible. Yet, I can't seem to stay away. Please, forgive me." Jason turned to walk away.

"Don't do this to me, Jason. Don't keep playing with my feelings."

"I'm sorry. All my fault."

He walked away.

His exit left Rachel wondering what exactly had just taken place. They'd been bantering with each other as usual, and then suddenly he grew sullen and was gone.

What had she done?

*****

Damn! He shouldn't have been teasing with her back and forth. He had no right. She relocated here to find a husband, and that man wasn't him, no matter how much they had enjoyed each other's kisses on the voyage. Guilt assuaged him when he thought of the way he treated her. He hadn't been thinking of her at all. Only himself.

Here was reality. Now he was back to being faithful to his late wife, to being lonely. He'd already had his chance at love and happiness, now it was someone else's time. But, Lord, he wanted her. Her bright spirit called to him as no other ever had including Cassie's. But he'd promised Cassie on her dying bed that he'd love her forever, and he would keep that promise.

Jason closed his eyes and willed himself to go to work in the trees. Logging. Cutting down trees, sending them down the river to the mill, that was what he needed now. Work.

He took one last look at Rachel. She wore her pink gingham dress today. She'd told him she thought it the most dignified of her dresses.

She directed the brides to the dormitories, but she stopped and looked over at him.

Could she read his mind and know he was watching her?

Then she sighed, looked down and went back to her duties.

Duty. That's what he was doing…his duty by his dead wife. This allegiance is what she would want, isn't it? Isn't that what he promised her after she'd passed? Cassie had been a good, caring woman, why would she want him to be miserable. He'd made those promises. She hadn't asked for them. All she'd asked for as she lay dying was for him to take care of their son and not to mourn her for too long. But how long was too long? He would always love Cassie, but he could also be with Rachel, couldn't he? He had some thinking to do.

*****

"I've been robbed!" shouted Bertha Corrigan. "My pearl earrings are missing."

"Me, too," wailed Nancy Picozzi. "My mother's brooch is gone."

"Settle down. Settle down." Rachel stood on the porch of building one, waving her arms up and down to get order. "I want everyone to finish unpacking and go through everything. I want you to tell Lucy what is missing. Lucy, see if there is paper, pen and ink in the kitchen. Make a list of every missing item and who it belonged to."

"All right," said Lucy, pointing at Dormitory One. "Everyone come back here and I'll get your information down. I'll be in a swing on the porch."

Jason ran up, looking worried.

"I heard shouts. What's the matter?"

Rachel's heart started pounding at the sight of him. Would it always be that way? She stood on the second step up into Dormitory One and was only slightly taller than Jason.

"The brides are missing things. So far just jewelry that we know of. They're going through all their belongings and we'll make a list."

"What do you propose to do after that?"

"Make a list of the usual suspects—one or more of the other brides or some of the ship's crew. I need you to make sure that Clancy doesn't leave until we have this mystery solved. I also need a list of the crew members. I want to make sure I don't miss anyone. Do you have a policeman or someone from the law that we can report this to?"

"Yes. Sheriff Brand Kearney. How do you know what to do? I thought you worked in a factory before becoming a bride."

"I did, but I've always wanted to be a detective and worked on a couple of cases in

New Bedford."

"I'll go get him while you continue this." He waved toward the brides searching their things.

"All right. I have to go through my trunk, too."

Rachel opened her trunk and quickly dug to the bottom where she had a small jewelry box. Her hand closed over the box, brought it up and opened it.

Lucy returned paper and pen in hand.

Rachel's hand formed a fist, and she gritted her teeth. I will not shout. "My grandmother's necklace is missing. Who could be doing this? I can't imagine it's one of the brides, but I don't know most of them very well. How well do you get to know a hundred people in three months?"

Lucy nodded. "I know. This will be difficult. You should let their law enforcement—the sheriff—take care of it."

Rachel looked at her dearest friend. "I know I probably should, but I can go places he can't and vice versa."

Lucy shook her head. "I don't know...you could get in lots of trouble, Rachel."

"Don't worry, Lucy. I can handle it."

Lucy cocked her head to one side and dipped her chin. "Like you did the Robertson affair? That was a disaster."

Rachel waved her hand to the side. "That was a fluke. How was I supposed to know that it was Mrs. Robertson that was having the affair and that she'd hired me to make her look innocent?"

"You would have if you'd been a real detective, but you're not, no matter how much you want to be." Lucy placed her hand on Rachel's arm. "Honey, you're a farm girl who went to work in the factory making dresses. Goodness, we'd never have met if you hadn't come to work there."

"I know." Rachel's shoulders sagged. "But I want to be a detective. I think I'd be good at it."

"And I think you'd be terrible at it. You jump to conclusions before all the evidence is in. A real detective doesn't do that."

Rachel frowned. She'd heard this from her before, and Lucy had reason to believe what she did. "I have a few things to work on—"

Lucy threw up her hands. "A few! Rachel. Has any case you've worked on turned out the way you thought it would…once all the evidence was in, of course."

Rachel looked to the right and then rolled her eyes to the left. She gazed anywhere but at Lucy. "Well, no, but—"

"No buts. Leave this to the professionals."

Rachel took a deep breath. *Lucy's right. I'm not a good detective, but I really think I could be. I'll simply not mention it to her again if I can help it.* "You're probably right."

Lucy dropped her chin and looked at Rachel. "You know I'm right."

Rachel nodded but looked over at the brides, watching them as they searched through their trunks to see if anything was missing.

She went from dormitory to dormitory and had the women go through their trunks.

Many of the brides were missing jewelry, but none of the missing items were found in any of the trunks.

This was a definite mystery and Rachel was determined to solve it and do it right this time. No jumping to conclusions. She'd consider only the actual evidence. Nothing else.

CHAPTER 4

A week later as she stood at the bottom of the steps of Dormitory One, Rachel looked over at Jason. He looked up at her, just as he was tackled by a young boy, with blond hair wearing a plaid shirt and brown wool pants.

His son? Of course, that must be Billy.

Jason ruffled the boy's hair and engulfed him in a bear hug.

Watching them, she could easily tell they loved each other.

Would she ever have a son who would hug her like that? Or a daughter, maybe? As the lump in her throat formed she swallowed it down.

Jason and the boy walked toward her. She stood straighter, putting her shoulders back and clasping her hands in front of her in what she hoped was a relaxed stance.

"Billy, this is Miss Rachel Sawyer. She's the unofficial leader of the brides. If you should need anything from the brides,

Miss Sawyer can probably get it."

Rachel held out her hand to Billy.

He reluctantly took it.

"Hi."

Billy looked up at his father and then at her and quickly withdrew his hand.

He knows. How could he know just from Jason introducing me?

"I'm very pleased to meet you, Billy. I've heard a lot about you. Your father is very proud of you for your reading and especially your curious mind. "

He looked up at his dad and smiled.

"You are?"

"Of course, I am." He threw his arm around Billy's shoulders and hugged the boy close. "I'm very proud to have you as my son."

Billy glowed.

I must remember to tell Jason to compliment Billy more often. What am I thinking? I have no reason to tell Jason anything. I should stay away from Jason but I can't seem to.

"Well, if you both will excuse me, I have to get back to the brides and finding the thief."

"Miss Sawyer, shouldn't you leave that

to the sheriff?" asked Jason. "He'll have this all sorted out in short order."

Rachel crossed her arms over her chest and cocked a brow. "Is that your way of telling me it's not women's work?"

Jason cleared his throat. "Uh, no, not really. I just think you should let the sheriff do his job."

Rachel nodded. "All right. I'll stop being so aggressive in my pursuits, provided he takes this seriously."

"I'm sure he will. Brand is a good man and a good sheriff."

"Can I go now, Dad?" asked Billy.

Jason dropped his arm from Billy's shoulders. "Sure. Where will you be?"

"Fishing with Leroy Jones at the beaver pond." He pointed up the hill.

"All right. Catch lots, and we'll have a fish fry for dinner."

Billy grinned. "Yes, sir." He ran off fast, kicking up dirt and bits of mud with each step.

She smiled. "He's a fine young man, Jason."

"I like to think so. I'm hoping Miss Doris Palmer, will be able to teach him more than I can. He has such a curious mind. I don't think he'll be a logger like his father."

"Does that disappoint you?"

"No, not at all. I want him to pursue his passion. Right now that is astronomy. I got him a telescope while we were in New Bedford. His birthday is just a week from now. He'll be ten."

She saw a shadow cross his face and sadness filled her as she realized the reason.

"You're remembering Cassie."

"Yes."

He said the single word softly.

Rachel knew the memories caused him pain and she laid a hand on his arm. "Jason, if she was as good a person as you say she was, do you really believe that she'd want you to remain alone forever? I can't believe that. She would want you to be happy."

"I don't know. I've some thinking to do."

"I can't wait forever."

He tucked an errant strand of hair behind her ear. "No, I don't suppose you can."

She grinned. "But, I do have a thief to catch."

He chuckled and shook his head. "Why do I believe you will?"

"I'll need your help. I want each of the

berths on the ship checked fully, including under the mattress and in the pillowcase if they have one. I don't know what kind of bedding the sailors have."

"That's already being done."

"Oh…well that's good." She felt like some of the wind had been knocked out of her sail as she heard that someone else had thought of checking the berths first.

"What else?"

Thrilled at his vote of confidence, she smiled. "I'll need to talk to each crew member and every bride—"

"That's also being done now by Sheriff Kearney. The interviews are taking place at Dolly's Saloon. It generally serves as the meeting place in town for whatever from interviews like this to a theater when a performing company comes through."

"Oh." Her shoulders sagged but then she straightened. "Do you think the sheriff would mind if I sat in on a few? The responses will be pretty much the same for everyone except the bride or sailor who is the perpetrator."

"Or possibly one of each working together."

She tapped her finger on her chin.

"That's a definite possibility. You could be good at this detective thing. Did you pick up any new seamen when you came to New Bedford?"

"We did. Three new sailors signed on. I never got acquainted with them, so you'd have to ask Clancy if you want to learn anything about them before they talk to the sheriff."

She lifted her eyebrow. "I bet one of them is the guilty party. Well, why don't you show me the town while we look for Clancy?"

"I can tell you exactly where Clancy is and this," he swept his hand wide in front of him. "This is the whole town, pretty much."

He walked with her in a semi-circle around the dock area, about two blocks wide and three blocks long. He put his hands in his pockets, she thought to keep from touching her. Side by side they strolled leisurely in the dirt-covered street.

"You know walking with me like this is likely to spur rumors."

Rachel smiled and looked up at him. "We're not even holding hands. I think I'll take my chances."

She hadn't been this close to him in the

daytime, even on the ship, just their stolen kisses on the boat, in the dark. Being with him now, reminded her of Ezra. How long had it been since she'd walked arm-in-arm with a man? Ezra was the last man she'd been this close to and he died in 1861, four years ago. Four years was a long time to be alone.

Jason had been alone even longer. Cassie died ten years ago and he was still alone. Rachel would change that if he'd let her, but she wasn't sure he would. After their last night aboard the ship, she was surprised that he wanted to show her the town. Was he as affected by their relationship on the ship as she was? Was he unable to keep away from her, just as she was him?

"First, on our left the plain wooden building the dock master's shack."

"It's much nicer than any shack I ever saw."

"You're correct. It's a nice three-room cabin, but it's just called a shack."

"I see."

"The white two-story building next to this is Dolly's Saloon. She lives in the rooms above. Dolly is a sweetheart, and I know you'll come to love her."

The buildings all look like new. Did they get a fresh coat of paint because we were coming?

"I'm anxious to meet Dolly. Clancy has nothing but good things to say about her."

Jason laughed. "Yes, Clancy has somewhat of a crush on our Dolly, but it's well deserved. She's a good woman."

"Oh, I think that's so sweet."

Jason chuckled.

She would have sworn he started to reach for her.

He carried on. "I'm not surprised you think so. I believe most women are romantics at heart. You'll find that Dolly has a heart of gold. I'm sure you and the other ladies will come to call her a very good friend."

"I agree we are romantic. Dolly sounds like a wonderful lady, despite owning a saloon." Her father frequented a saloon, and her mother was none too happy about that situation. Owning and running one sounded scandalously inappropriate, but she wouldn't hold that against Dolly. Besides, everything she'd read about saloons made them seem like a good place to perhaps find more cases to investigate.

"Next, the big red building holds the mercantile, mail office and the new telegraph office. They are all run and owned by Fred Longmire and his wife June. A nicer couple you couldn't find. I'm sure you'll be meeting them soon. They have a new baby girl named Ruth, who they love to show to everyone. She's their first child."

"Oh, a new baby, how wonderful. I'm sure that at some point in time the ladies will have things for him to order in."

This town is so small. I know Suzanne told us it was but I never expected it to be this small. I have a hard time imagining that this one store is all they have. In New Bedford, we had a milliner for hats, a shoemaker for shoes and other shops for different things. Clothes from a seamstress or a dressmaker. And what about a grocer? Are we really supposed to grow our food? Will we all be able to get used to it? What choice do we have? And Jason is so proud of his town.

"Well, he can do it. We can get just about anything, but it takes time for them to be shipped in. Living here is not like back east. You can't just walk down to your local milliner and pick up a new hat."

Was he reading my mind? Living here is like being back on the farm. We had to order things there, too. Wilton Falls was a small town but compared to Seattle, Wilton Falls was a thriving metropolis. "I understand. I'm sure all of my ladies are aware that we are not in New Bedford any longer. This reminds me of the little town I grew up near, though Wilton Falls was bigger than Seattle."

A wagon passed by them sending clods of dirt up in its wake. Jason walked on the street side, so none of the mud reached Rachel.

"Hi, Jason. Glad to see you back. Is that one of our brides?" The question was asked by a middle-aged man with brown hair that was thinning on top.

"Hi, Ralph. Yes, this is Miss Rachel Sawyer."

"Nice to meet you, Ralph."

The man took Rachel's hand in his and placed a kiss on the top.

"I'm real happy to meet you, Miss Sawyer. Would you mind if I called on you this evening."

"Ah, Ralph, that won't be possible. Miss

Sawyer is still unpacking and has a meeting scheduled with the other brides tonight."

The man looked back and forth between Rachel and Jason. Then he cocked his head, narrowed his eyes and smiled. "I see the way of things. That's all right. I got ninety-nine more ladies to ask to court."

He bowed his head toward Rachel and walked away whistling.

"Are all the men in town as affable as Ralph?"

"Many are. Some are not. There's a mix of personalities like anywhere else."

They heard a screech and then the hiss of a cat, followed by a yellow streak being chased by a dog with gray fur.

Rachel laughed. "It's a good thing that cat is fast. I don't think that dog was very happy with the cat."

"No one is happy with that particular cat. The animal likes to yowl in the middle of the night and is forever picking on the other animals in town."

"Shall we continue the tour?"

"Of course. This road leading out of town will take you by the mill owned by Alfred Pope, arguably the richest man in town, if you listen to him. To the right of the road, you find first the butcher, Leland Murray, in the green single-story building. He has arrangements with a local rancher and gets us the beef that we need. Several of the lumberjacks hunt as well and sell some of the meat to Leland, so he'll offer elk, deer, even bear on occasion."

She stopped, her eyes wide. *This really is the wild frontier.* "Bear? Who in the world would eat bear?"

"Most any of us. The meat tastes a lot like venison, but sweeter and it has a texture like pork which we don't get. So far, no one has decided to raise pigs nearby. When we go to Olympia, we can get pork and often order it for dinner when we make the trip."

"Do you have to stay overnight when you make those trips?"

"Yes, when we go for supplies, we have the wagon and we're much slower than a rider on a horse is. That's why we only go once every other month or so. We can do the trip there and back on a horseback in one day. "

"What about when the brides want something?"

He thought about it for a moment.

"I suppose we'd have to get a list from

them and then we could fill it."

She shook her head.

"That won't always suffice. Sometimes I, or some other bride of your choice, will have to accompany you."

He lifted his eyebrows and pursed his lips. "Well, I suppose if you have to, we'll work out something, so it's appropriate for you to do so."

"Thank you for not saying 'no' outright."

"I try to be accommodating." He pointed at the next building. "There, we have the sheriff's office and behind it his house. It's not large, but he seems to like it. Next to that is the Seattle Inn. Lastly is the bakery. Most of us get our bread and other baked goods from Mr. and Mrs. Jones first thing in the morning. That's why you don't smell baking bread now. She's already done her baking for the day. The other three children in town belong to the Jones'. And then south of the bakery are your dormitories. And there you have all of Seattle."

"Not hardly. Where do you work and live?"

"Not in town. You follow that road." He pointed at a set of wagon ruts headed up the mountain. "For about half a mile to where it forks. The house is there on the right. Follow the right fork up the mountain, and you'll find the logging camp."

I'm disappointed that he'll be so far away after the closeness we shared on the ship for three months, but does that really matter? Nothing can come of our time together anyway. "It doesn't sound like it would be a nice stroll up there."

"No. I would describe it as more of a hike since it is all uphill, but coming back into town is nice because it's all downhill."

"I suppose if I want you to come for tea, you'll have to come to the dormitory." She pointed up the hill toward his home. "I can't come to you."

He stopped and looked down at her, lifted his hand and brought the knuckle of his right index finger along her jawline.

"Don't invite me for tea or anything else, I'll likely not be able to refuse, and you know nothing can come of it."

"No, I don't know. I know you have to 'do some thinking' about what Cassie would want for you and I think you'll realize she wants you to be happy. Don't I make you happy, Jason?"

"Yes, more than I have a right to feel."

Taking what little courage she had left, she tried to make him understand. "No. That's not true. You deserve happiness, maybe more than most because you've been alone for so long. Let me help you. Let me into your life."

"I don't see how I can. What about Billy?"

"What about him? He'll get used to me. He might even love me eventually. You might even love me…eventually."

She felt him stiffen and knew she'd lost the fight. Lost him.

His lips flattened into a straight line. "Just because we are content, doesn't mean we love each other. Billy is the only one I have room in my heart for right now. Remember that."

Rachel closed her eyes, trying to keep her tears at bay. She took a step back. "I couldn't forget if I wanted to. I'm sure you'll remind me often enough."

He clenched his fists. "Rachel, I…I—"

The sinking feeling in her stomach told her this was it. The end. "No, you're right Jason. I need to remember you're off limits to me, at least your heart is. I have to decide if that's all right with me and right now I don't know. Thank you for showing me the town."

Rachel turned toward the dormitory and went inside. She didn't look back once.

*****

Jason watched her go. Why couldn't he leave well enough alone and let her think he loved her? Because he was an honorable man and that was not an honorable act. Honesty was needed because if they didn't have that, then they didn't have anything.

What *would* Cassie have wanted? He'd been alone for almost ten years. In all these years he'd never wanted to be with anyone else, and maybe that was why he was having such a hard time with Rachel. Because he wanted to be with her. He was tired of being alone and wanted to share his life with someone special. With Rachel.

Jason suspected Rachel was right. Cassie was a good-hearted woman, and she wouldn't have wanted him to be alone. Jason made his promise when he was overcome with grief and Cassie had already passed. If she'd been alive she'd have told him that his promise was ridiculous.

Billy was old enough for Jason to have a

relationship of his own. He knew from experience that he only had five or six years before Billy would want to take off on his own.

Was now the right time? Was Rachel the right woman? And if the answer was yes, had he made such a mess of the situation already that she wouldn't forgive him?

Jason had a lot of things to think about. What he needed was some time alone. He walked home and filled his pack with a couple of blankets and food for tonight and tomorrow's breakfast. If he stayed away for longer than that his brothers and Billy would begin to worry, so he left them a note.

Family,

I need time away from everyone to think through some things. Gentlemen, please watch Billy for me.

Billy, I love you, son. Mind your uncles.

Dad

*****

Jason walked up the mountain to the highest lake. They named it Lake Cassie, after his wife. He often came here when he wanted to feel close to her.

Now was one of those times.

He set up his tent and built a small

campfire. Then he sat and talked to his dead wife.

"Hi, Cassie. I don't know what to do. I don't know what you'd want. I found someone I want to marry. I don't love her as I did you, but we like each other, and until Rachel, I've never been attracted to anyone since you."

He stirred the fire, placing the stir stick on the ground outside of the fire ring he'd built from large rocks. Then leaned back against the log he'd camped beside.

"I don't know what to do. Billy's done well without a mother, but it would be good for him to have one, nonetheless. He'd learn how to treat a woman, respect for them and to cherish them."

Jason closed his eyes and tried to picture Cassie. She looked a lot like Rachel with golden hair and blue eyes. Rachel is curvier than Cassie was. She hadn't even needed a corset, just a chemise. And her face...he could still see her smile and hear her laugh on nights like this one, where it was so quiet not even a cricket chirped.

Tugging his watch from his front pants pocket, he flipped open the cover, and by the light from the fire, he gazed at the picture of himself and Cassie. Smiling, he remembered the day the photograph was taken. Getting Cassie to stop smiling so the photographer could take the picture was quite a task. She was having too much fun at the fair. Going to the fair was their first outing as a married couple, and she'd taken advantage of that fact…holding his hand as they watched a pie eating contest and wound their way through all the animals being displayed. When they reached the baby animals, she'd squealed and released his hand so she could pick up a tiny gray kitten.

The owner of the kittens was giving them away, and that was how they acquired Cloudy. Cassie'd named the kitten that because she said he looked like the sky on a cloudy day. They'd had the cat for nearly nine years. The animal died just before they realized Cassie was pregnant. She'd cried for days over that cat.

All the memories came flooding back and in not one of them was Cassie anything but kind and giving. She worked hard to make sure those around her were happy.

Finally, he remembered the night she died. Jason had held her in his arms while she held Billy. Suddenly she began to cry.

"Don't mourn me too long. Be happy and give Billy a mama. He deserves to have a mother's love, too."

"No. I promise I won't marry again. You're my wife and will always be my wife."

She hadn't heard him but died with her last words.

Jason had been wrong. He mourned her too long. Just what she'd asked him not to do. He would always love Cassie. She was his first love. But he could also marry Rachel. He might not love her, but they liked each other enough to make a good marriage. Jason was finally doing what Cassie wanted him to. Be happy. Rachel made him happy.

CHAPTER 5

Rachel thought she might know who the thief was but she wanted to make sure before she leveled any accusations. Lucy was right; she tended to jump to conclusions that usually proved wrong. When Rachel was sure, she'd tell the sheriff but not before.

Ten days after she and Jason took the tour of the town, Rachel was crossing the muddy street from Dolly's to the dormitory. The time was early morning, and she'd taken Dolly some sewing and picked up more clothes to mend. She suddenly noticed Jason Talbot walking purposefully toward her.

A man came out of the mercantile.

"Jason. I need to talk to you about those axes."

"Not now, Fred."

Jason kept walking.

She kept walking, too. He couldn't be coming to see her, could he? Rachel held her skirts high, juggled the parcel of clothes from Dolly and made a dash for the dormitory. Jason was faster and cut off her exit.

"Rachel. We have to talk."

Though it pained her, she knew talking was futile. "I doubt there is anything that we need to say to each other."

She moved to go around him.

He blocked her.

"Rachel. We need some privacy."

She waved her hand taking in the stair she stood on and the porch of the dormitory. "This is as private as you, and I get. If you have something to say, then say it."

"Very well, if that is what you wish."

He dropped to one knee, heedless of the mud, and looked up at her.

"Rachel Sawyer, will you do me the great honor of becoming my wife?"

Her mouth opened but no words came out, and she began to cry. How could he do this to her? Make her believe...did she believe? Would Jason love her? Was she willing to accept that he might not? " Jason, I—"

"Please, Rachel, marry me. We're good together. You know we are, and we can be even better if you marry me."

Rachel looked down at the man she

loved, saw his vulnerability and knew then she'd say yes.

"Rach?" he asked softly.

"Yes. I'll marry you."

Jason stood, took her into his arms and lowered his head meeting her lips with his and kissing her thoroughly.

Rachel wrapped her arms around his neck, kissing him back with all the love in her heart. She hoped it was enough for her to be the only one in the relationship who was in love.

Clapping forced them to their senses and they broke apart.

Jason kept his arm around her waist holding her by his side.

Rachel grinned up at him.

"Have you told Billy?"

"No, I'll tell them all tonight at dinner. Would you like to come to dinner, or perhaps tomorrow night instead after they know?"

She couldn't keep the smile off her face. Her dreams were coming true. "I'd love to come to dinner tonight. I don't believe any of your brothers want anything but your happiness."

He leaned back, still with his arm around

her, and furrowed his brows.

"Billy, on the other hand, may be a bit of a problem."

She cocked her head and peered up at him. "Why would he have a problem with you marrying me?"

He gazed down at her, covering her hand with his. "Look at this from his point of view. He's had me all to himself for ten years, and now there's this woman who wants to take me away."

She shook her head. "I'm not taking you anywhere."

"No, not physically. Emotionally. He's only ten and never had to share me with anyone except his uncles."

"Together I think we can reassure him that I'm not taking his place in your heart."

She felt him stiffen at her mention of the heart. His reaction was expected. Jason still didn't realize he loved her, but she was sure he did. *He just had to.*

"So when will you collect me for dinner? Are we walking or will you bring a horse or buggy?"

"I don't want you to be out of breath by the time you get to the house so I thought I'd drive down and get you in the buggy."

"Thank you, kind sir; I had no desire to walk up to your home either."

"How about taking a walk with me in the woods? No hills, I promise. Just some much-needed privacy."

"I'd like to talk to you in private, too. I think I might know who the thief is."

He took her by the hand and led her away into the nearby forest. It wasn't too long before the town could no longer be seen or heard. The only sounds were their breathing and the occasional bird chirping. After a short walk, Jason led her to a downed tree where they could sit.

He held her hand in his.

"Are you still working on that mystery?"

"Yes. All these women came here with little more than the clothes on their backs and maybe one or two pieces of precious jewelry. They deserve to get them back. And I want my grandmother's locket back. That necklace is all I have left of her."

"All right, who do you think did it?"

"Well, I have two suspects. Glynnis Harte didn't even open her trunk like the other women did when they were told to check and make sure they had all of their belongings."

"That doesn't prove anything. Maybe she knew she didn't have anything valuable to take."

"True and that's what I thought too until she started meeting one of the sailors from the ship. He meets her behind Dolly's, and they are there for only a few minutes. She pulls something from her reticule, and he gives her something that she puts in her bag."

"That still doesn't mean—"

Rachel nodded. "I agree. The other woman I suspect is Nicole Wescott. She's been buying things at the mercantile...lots of things...dress material, a new corset, and new shoes. None of that's cheap. Where did she get the money? Women with money don't become mail-order brides."

"It does sound like you have reasons to be suspicious. Have you told Sheriff Kearney? Do you have any proof against either woman?"

"No, and I didn't want to go to him without something more substantial. He'll say all the same things that you are, but I don't know if I can convince him...he doesn't want to marry me."

Jason smiled and pulled her close.

"You're right about that. I'd have to shoot him if he did."

He lowered his head and took her lips with his, entering her mouth with his tongue, tasting her as she tasted him.

Rachel smiled. She loved the way he kissed. Ezra had never kissed her as Jason did. And Jason smelled good, like sandalwood, her favorite scent for a man.

He broke away but kept his arm around her shoulders.

"You're smiling. Why?"

"I was just thinking about your kisses and how much I enjoy them." She continued to smile at her memories.

"Good. That's the way it should be between two people who are getting married."

Her smile faltered. "Of course, you're right."

Why was she a little sad that he didn't say 'between two people in love'? She had to have hope that he would change his mind someday. That belief is what kept her going forward.

"Rachel." He held her with his arm loose around her shoulders. "I don't want you following those women anymore. If you're right, you could be hurt."

She frowned. "What brought that on?"

His expression grew serious. "Now that you've agreed to marry me, I think you should be more careful of yourself and the things you do."

She turned a bit, and he placed both arms around her. Rachel slammed her fist into her hand. "You don't understand. I can't let Glynnis or Nicole, whichever one is the thief, get away with stealing from me and the other brides. Some of these women like me have lost both their parents or grandparents. That necklace or bracelet or earrings are all we have to remember our mothers or grandmothers. For the other women, that piece of jewelry might be all they had to keep them from being destitute. They'll be forced to marry even if they don't want to, even if they don't find someone to love. Don't you understand this woman is taking away their lives?"

"I don't want you to be hurt. You must stop. I demand it."

She shrugged off his arm and stood, forcing him to release her. Rachel backed away onto the path they'd followed into the forest.

Placing her hands on her hips. "You demand it? How dare you demand anything from me?"

He rose and mimicked her stance. "I dare because I'm worried about you. I can't bear to see you injured."

She looked up at him, saw his furrowed brows and pursed lips and realized he cared. He may not love her, not yet, but he cared. She was gratified he did.

"Jason. I have to see this through. The women depend on me. If you want to keep me safe, then help me. Find out whatever you can about this sailor she meets. His name is Harvey Long."

He looked down at her.

A frown marred his handsome face.

"All right. I'll find out what I can, but until I talk to you tomorrow, I don't want you to do anything else. Just give me a day to get the answers you seek."

She nodded, and her heart leaped. "I'll give you a day but tomorrow night I'll follow her again. I'm determined, Jason. I won't let this stealing get swept under the rug."

"I understand, and I agree. The thievery has to stop. Can we talk about something else now?"

"Like what?"

"Like when do you want to get married? Isn't that something the bride usually decides?"

Excitement filled her. Her dreams were coming true. She would have the family she craved. "I don't know, I've never been a bride before, but I see no need to wait. We've known each other for months now, and we know what we want. So let's do it as soon as possible, besides Lucy is ready to be my maid of honor."

He frowned. "How did she know I'd be proposing? I didn't even know until today. Oh, by the way." He reached into his pocket and pulled out a small box. "This is for you."

Rachel took the box from his outstretched hand. She'd pictured this scene many times over the years, and the man had always placed the ring on her finger. She handed the box back to him.

"Will you open it and put the ring on my finger, please?"

Jason lifted an eyebrow and flipped the small black box open. Inside was the most exquisite diamond ring she'd ever seen.

Jason took the ring from the box and put it on the third finger of her left hand, kissed it and then kissed her.

"Do you like it?"

"I love it." *And you.* She kissed him and then held up her hand and admired the ring. "I think we should get married one week from this coming Saturday which will be May sixth. That gives Lucy and me time to make sure our dresses are clean and pressed, our hair done and whatever else we think of along the way."

"All right. The sixth it is."

He put an arm around her shoulders and turned her, so they stood chest to chest.

She loved the feel of his chest against her body.

"I will wait most anxiously." He leaned down and kissed her lips. "To get you into my bed."

Rachel loved his flirting. She grinned, giddy with excitement. The thought of making love with Jason didn't make her afraid. Her memories were just that and didn't seem to intrude when she was with him. She knew she was safe. He would protect her at all costs.

"And I to be there. What about our

wedding night? Do you propose to spend it at your house?"

His eyelids closed halfway, and his voice was low. "I thought we would go to Olympia for a couple of days. That way I can keep you in bed all day, and no one will think twice about my doing so because they will know we're newlyweds."

She felt the heat rise through her and knew that if they were not in the shadow of the trees, he would see she was bright red with embarrassment. She'd never had such a frank talk with anyone much less a man, but she must remember this man was to be her husband, and he was right, she shouldn't think anything odd about it.

"Won't they know that here?"

"Yes, but they'd expect us to go about our regular daily chores, and I don't intend to do that."

"You know, this conversation is highly irregular."

"My darling, Rachel, nothing, and I mean *nothing,* is highly irregular or forbidden between a husband and a wife."

"Very well, we'll go to Olympia. But doesn't that mean we'll spend our wedding night on the ground? Don't we have to camp overnight?"

He gently placed a stray strand of hair behind her ear.

"We do, one night, but I promise we'll be comfortable. We won't be on the ground. I'll bring plenty of blankets to pad the wagon under us and to put over us, but you and I will be keeping each other warm."

"Jason, I trust you. Now kiss me and let us get back before gossip gets started. Besides, I have to visit Mrs. Jones, the baker, about a wedding cake."

He lifted an eyebrow. "We *must* have a cake."

He grinned and then took her face between his palms, pressed his lips to hers. Slow, deliberate, he parted his lips, and his tongue darted out into her mouth where they played with each other until they were both breathless. He pulled back and rested his forehead against hers.

He'd kissed her, sipped from her like she was fine wine. "I don't think I could ever get tired of kissing you."

She was breathless as she spoke. He always managed to do that to her. "That's a good thing because I'm the last woman you'll ever kiss if you know what's good for you."

"Feisty little thing aren't you."

Her grip on his jacket tightened. "I protect what is mine, Jason Talbot and from now on, you are mine and so is Billy."

"I'm glad you include him."

She leaned back in his arms. "Of course, I do. He's your son. I want him to like me but whether he does or not, I will still protect him."

"You're a marvelous woman, Rachel. I…I care for you very much."

"And I you." *I'll take your caring, for now, but I hope that love will soon follow.* "Now let's go back. Lucy will be beside herself wanting to see my ring."

They made their way back to town holding hands. She thought Jason might not want to hold hands, it was a bit unseemly, but he seemed to enjoy the feeling as much as she did.

He escorted her to the dormitory.

"I'll be here at six o'clock tonight to pick you up for dinner. Now I need to talk to Fred about some axes."

"I'll be ready."

She leaned up and kissed him lightly on the lips.

He grinned, winked, and let her be, whistling as he walked away.

Rachel went up the dormitory steps and was nearly run over by Lucy.

"I heard you accepted Jason's proposal. Oh, Rachel, I'm so happy for you. When is the date? Let me see your ring."

Lucy lifted Rachel's left hand.

"Oh, my gosh, that's beautiful."

"Thank you." Rachel admired the ring on her finger. "I think so, too. Jason has good taste." She gazed at her friend. "How did you know? Who told you?"

"Of course, he does. He's marrying you, isn't he? As to who told us, it was Daisy. She saw the whole thing. I came out to see you, but you and Jason were headed to the forest." Lucy lifted her brows. "For some privacy? Hmm?"

Rachel chuckled.

"Yes, we wanted some privacy. The date is a week from Saturday on May 6th. I just wanted to make sure everything, like our dresses, were ready."

Lucy furrowed her brows. "You know mine is and yours is, too. So why the delay?"

Rachel closed her eyes and sighed, her

stomach in knots. "I'm nervous Lucy. I'll know more after dinner tonight."

"Come. Sit on the swing with me."

They retired to the porch swing.

"Now what are you nervous about? Jason loves you—"

"No, he doesn't." Rachel shook her head. "In his mind, he can't love anyone but his dead wife, Cassie. If he does, he thinks he's disloyal to her memory."

Lucy frowned. "If that's true, why are you marrying him?"

Rachel felt the tears leak in a slow trickle down her cheek and looked at her lap. "Because I love him. I could never marry anyone else, even if Jason doesn't love me. At least this way, I have a chance for children of my own as well as helping him raise Billy."

Lucy placed her arm around Rachel's shoulders and hugged her.

"I understand. Truly I do. Unrequited love is the worst thing in the world. You see I feel the same way about Drew Talbot, but he doesn't know I'm alive."

Rachel swiped at her tears. "Oh, Lucy. I'm so sorry.'

"To make matters worse, whenever I'm

around him I'm clumsy. I mean really clumsy. Running into things and knocking things over like a bull in a china shop."

"You're just nervous around him because you like him. It's too bad we can't get you not to care one way or the other."

"I can't not care. I love him. I can't pretend."

"How do you feel when you see him with other women? Are you still clumsy or just angry?"

"Just angry."

"I suppose you could try to stay angry at Drew until he discovers the real you."

Lucy shook her head.

"As soon as he's gone, I'm not angry anymore, and I'm not clumsy either, as long as he's not around."

"He needs to see you being your regular self, but you can't know that he's watching. I'll have to see what I can do."

"I don't know how you can do it so I don't know he's watching. I always seem to know when he's around and then I proceed to walk into a wall or fall over a chair or who knows what else." Lucy sighed. "By the time I get control of myself, he's gone."

Rachel took Lucy's hand in hers. "Look,

I'm having dinner with Jason and his family tonight. Maybe he'll have an idea."

Lucy's eyes shot wide.

"Oh, no. You mustn't. I don't want Jason to know what an idiot I am."

"First, you are not an idiot. Second, I'll stress to Jason the delicateness of the situation. He'll be glad to help."

CHAPTER 6

Jason was not glad to help. He stood across the porch from her with his arms crossed over his chest and a frown on his face

"You want me to help you fool my brother? I won't do it."

They stood on the far end of the full porch that fronted the Talbot home, getting some private time before dinner.

"You're not fooling him. Just helping him to see Lucy the way she is when she's not nervous. Drew makes her nervous."

"No. Absolutely not."

She closed the gap between them and put a hand on his arm. "Please, Jason. I'm not asking you to do anything improper or to lure Drew to his doom. I just want him to see Lucy for herself."

He started to shake his head.

Never having been this forward before, she liked feeling safe enough to push for what she wanted. She placed her hands on either side of his face, holding him still. Then she stood on tiptoe and pressed her lips to his.

"Please."

She did *like* kissing the man and kissed him again.

"I don't—"

"Pretty please."

She kissed him again, this time letting her tongue explore the contours of the inside of his mouth.

Him playing with her tongue in return.

His arms came around her and pulled her close.

"You do make quite a case for Lucy."

She wound her arms around his neck. She liked that as an engaged couple they didn't have to hide in the dark any longer when they wanted to kiss.

"We're not tricking, Drew. I simply want Lucy to not be so nervous around him. If she can just be herself, all will be well. Trust me."

He shrugged his shoulders and tilted his head very slightly toward her. "Very well. I'll ask Dolly if we can borrow her window over the saloon balcony, assuming that Drew is interested in the first place."

"Of course. If Drew has absolutely no interest in her, then we won't go through with this. Heck, if Lucy thought Drew was interested in someone else, her nerves would calm because she'd know she had no chance."

"Let's worry about Lucy and Drew at another time."

He lowered his head and kissed her. By the time they broke apart, Rachel was weak in the knees and breathless.

"How is it you always do that to me?"

"Do what?"

"Leave me unable to stand on my own after we've kissed."

He grinned.

She could swear he puffed his chest a bit.

"I'm just that good, I guess."

"Hmpft. As an engaged woman, I won't be kissing any other men, so how will I know you're the best?"

"You'll just have to take my word for it."

Suddenly the screen door slammed, Billy looked over at them and cried out before running down the steps and into the forest.

She shook her head and closed her eyes. A tear escaped and rolled down her cheek. "I'd so hoped he'd accept me, but he hasn't—yet. I'm sure that eventually he will, but for now, we have to find him, Jason. He could get hurt."

Jason hugged her. "He'll come around with a little time. And he knows his way home. He's been in the woods after dark many times."

"But this situation is different. Billy's hurt, angry and feels betrayed. We have to find him and quickly. Is there someplace he would go?"

Jason furrowed his brows and looked toward the forest where Billy disappeared. "Perhaps you're right. We didn't get a chance to talk to him before he heard and saw us. There's a place that I take him fishing which isn't far but it's difficult to get to once you're off the main trail. Come with me. You can go part of the way. I think we should talk to him together."

"Agreed. I've got my coat on. Let's go."

Jason got two lanterns and they headed off into the forest along a wide, well-used path. They walked about ten minutes before he called a halt, for which Rachel was grateful. She'd had to practically run to keep up with Jason's long strides, but she hadn't wanted to ask him to slow down because they needed to find Billy.

"You can sit on that fallen tree just across the path from here and wait for us."

He pointed at the downed log and turned back to her.

"I'll bring him back."

"I have no doubt."

She lifted herself onto her toes and kissed him, just a short peck.

"Go. Go find your son."

She walked over to the log and sat watching the forest where Jason had entered it. *If I were a child, where would I go? Probably someplace where I'd feel safe and where I'd been before. The pond where he and Jason fished together is a good place to start.*

Rachel sat on the log for a good fifteen minutes, listening to the forest sounds, crickets chirping, the slight rustle of pines as the breeze blew through them and wondered about bears. Were there bears or other dangerous animals here in the forest? She shook her head. *Jason wouldn't leave me if there were a danger.*

"What are you doing here?"

Billy's voice came from behind her.

She shrieked, jumped up and was to the other side of the path before she stopped and looked back.

Putting a hand to her throat, she took several deep breaths before she could speak.

"Billy! You scared the crap out of me. Forgive my language."

"What are you doing here?"

He was on edge, nearly in tears; she heard it in his voice as it broke on the word 'here'.

"I'm waiting for your father. He went to your fishing place to find you."

He stood about ten feet from her, his arms straight at his sides, hands clenched into a fist. "Why don't you go back to where you came from? Me and Dad don't need you."

She winced at the pain she heard in his voice. "Billy. Your father caring for me doesn't mean he loves you any less."

"He's forgetting Mama."

Rachel hesitated, wondering if she should speak without Jason present. "No. He's not. He's doing what your mama would have wanted. She wouldn't have wanted him to be alone. He deserves some happiness."

"He's got me." Billy's voice cracked again, belying his tears.

"And he loves you very much, more than anything or anyone. But the heart is huge and can hold feelings for lots of people. *"I still love my grandparents even though they are gone.* Do you believe that your Dad can't love his brothers because he loves you?"

"No."

" Of course you don't." *He's listening. Maybe I'm changing his mind or at least have him questioning.* "You know that he loves them but in a different way. The same is true for your dad and me. He cares for me differently than he loves you." She moved a little closer to him. "You are the most important person in his world."

"She's right, son."

Jason walked out of the dark, his lantern extinguished.

Rachel jumped at the sound of his voice. "You two have got to stop sneaking up on me. You'll give me gray hair."

Billy ran to his father.

Jason quickly set down the lantern and

wrapped his arms around his crying son.

"I love you, Billy. No matter what, you are my son, my first born child. No one can ever take your place in my heart."

"I'm sorry, Dad."

"You've got nothing to be sorry about."

Jason held out his arm toward Rachel.

Relieved, she went to him and put her arms around him and Billy.

"I want Rachel to marry me, marry us, and she's said yes. Haven't you, Rachel?"

"Yes, to both of you. You're a package deal, and I want you both."

Billy looked up with watery eyes.

"You want us both?"

"Yes. I do. Very much."

He swiped his wet cheeks with the palms of his hands and smiled.

"We both want you, too." His voice broke again.

Rachel peered up at Jason, who wore a smile. He nodded.

"That's right Rachel, we do."

"Well, that's good, because I'm marrying you both. Now, what do you say we go back and see what your Uncle Adam has prepared for our dinner."

"Oh, I know," said Billy, hopping and

jumping along the path. "He got the last bear roast out of the ice house. He says this is a special dinner and deserves a special meat."

"Bear? Oh, my." She placed her hand on her throat.

Jason laughed.

*****

They walked back home with Billy leading the way, skipping and chattering, while Rachel and Jason followed, holding hands.

"I think he feels better." *I know I feel better with no more secrets.*

"He does. Thank you for taking the time to talk to him."

"Of course, I would. I want us to be friends. That won't happen unless we talk to each other."

"Beautiful and smart, too."

She cocked her head. "I'm glad you think so."

Jason chuckled.

"And modest, as well."

As they approached the tall three-story structure that would soon be her home, she saw that all her soon-to-be brothers-in-law were waiting for them on the porch.

She tried to let go of Jason's hand, but he

just tightened his grip.

Then he brought her hand to his mouth and kissed the top.

"Calm yourself. We're home."

She'd gotten the grand tour before they'd first gone outside and then looking for Billy. Rachel tried to relax, knowing that the vast log house would soon be her home, too. She would be responsible for cleaning the house which compared to her tiny room at the boarding house or even the big house on the farm where she'd grown up, was huge. These men were hopefully not as messy as her brothers had been.

One of the things she loved about the house was the window above the sink which looked out on the mountainside. She'd be able to look out while doing the dishes and Jason assured her she'd see more wild animals out that window than anywhere else in Seattle.

The second and third floors were all bedrooms. Eight in all. Michael, Gabe, Drew, and Billy had rooms on the third floor. Jason and Adam had bedrooms on the second floor, at opposite ends. A third bedroom, the one next to Adam's room was for storage. The fourth bedroom, the one next to Jason's room stood empty. Rachel thought she would ask if it could be the sewing room. She also wondered if he'd buy her a sewing machine. She could make all their clothes that way. Her work at the dress factory taught her a lot.

Adam waved his arm to bring them into the house. "About time you three got back. Dinner's gonna be cold."

"I'm sorry, Adam. My fault." Rachel flashed him a smile.

Billy looked over at her and cocked his head.

She took his hand and squeezed it.

He gave her a small smile.

If any of the brothers noticed, they didn't say anything.

The kitchen included the dining table with eight straight-backed chairs around it. Scroll-like carving on the top of the backs added to their beauty.

"Now that you've returned let's eat." Adam ushered them all inside while he held open the door.

Jason sat at one end and Adam at the other. Billy sat on Jason's left, Rachel on his right.

"Before we eat, I have an

announcement. Rachel has graciously agreed to become my wife and enter this crazy family."

"About time." Adam picked up the knife to carve the roast. "The way you've been holding hands and kissing, we wondered when you'd make an honest woman of her. And we were all ready to knock some sense into you if you didn't."

Jason sat and took Rachel's hand in his. "Now you don't have to, so let's eat."

Adam cut the roast into nice thick slices.

"I can't eat that much meat," said Rachel with an inward grimace. "I need about a quarter of that size."

"Certainly." He took one of the slices, cut it into quarters and placed a piece on her plate.

"Thank you." Her plate was passed back to her, and she gazed down at the delicious food. "Dinner looks marvelous, Adam. I can't wait to try everything." She picked up her knife and fork, cut a small bite of the roast and put it in her mouth. The taste was different than beef or pork but quite good nonetheless. Since she'd never had venison, she couldn't compare the bear roast to that. She swallowed. "Adam, this is delicious. I have to tell you, I was skeptical that I would like the bear meat, but I do. Thank you for educating me, whether you intended to or not."

"I'm glad you like it," said Adam. "We don't get company very often, so my cooking skills go mostly unnoticed by this group of savages."

"Oh, I'm sure they appreciate your efforts, they just forget to tell you so. Isn't that right gentlemen?"

All the brothers nodded.

"That's right Adam," Michael, the brother that most resembled Suzanne, with blond hair and blue eyes, reached over and punched his brother in the arm. "We do appreciate your cooking. It's the cleaning up we don't like."

Rachel shook her head. "No one likes doing dishes."

Adam appeared to be quite the cook. The offerings included salmon, fried potatoes, peas, and fresh bread in addition to the bear meat. For dessert, she saw a coconut cake just like the one she'd admired in the bakery window.

"I see that you all visit the Jones' bakery, too."

"Yes, I never learned to bake." Adam looked around, jutting his chin at his brothers. "None of these heathens did either."

"I love to bake." Rachel smiled delightedly that she had the skill to share. "Pies are my specialty. I haven't had time to bake anything here yet."

"We'll keep you baking pies until you don't ever want to see a pie again. You see we all love pies, but Mrs. Jones doesn't like to make them. Hates her crusts," said Drew as he scooped up a spoonful of peas from his plate.

"My crusts are the lightest, crispiest you'll find anywhere. Just you wait and see."

"We await your efforts with bated breath and empty stomachs, my dear," said Jason.

She laughed.

"There is no way your stomachs are empty...any of you. I saw you all take at least seconds if not thirds of everything. Adam, you'll have to teach me the amounts of food I need to cook to satisfy this hungry horde."

The men all laughed.

Jason stood.

"Would you like to take a walk, Miss Sawyer?" asked Jason.

"Why yes, I would, Mr. Talbot." Her gaze landed one by one on each of the men and the boy at the table. They all wore smiles—the same smile as Jason. They were definitely related.

She rose from the table and took Jason's offered arm as they walked out of the kitchen. Rachel heard the laughter from the room behind them.

"Why are they laughing?"

"Because they know the only reason I want to take a walk this late in the evening is so I can find some privacy to kiss you."

"Oh. You must think me very naïve."

"You are for now, but I'll teach you."

"Are there many things you will have to teach me?"

"Yes, there are."

He stopped and pointed to the sky. "We can no longer see the lights from the house, but the stars are glorious. There are the Milky Way and several constellations. See?"

His arm moved to indicate the shape of the The Big and Little Dippers, Orion, as well as the planet Venus.

"Venus is so very bright in the evening

sky, hence the name The Evening Star. Look." He was looking at her. "The moon overhead is nearly full, bathing us in silver light and making your dress shimmer like a golden coin. You are so beautiful."

"I like that you think so, but most of the men I knew thought I was plain."

"Never! You're lovely, and I shall never tire of telling you so."

Rachel giggled. "Spoken like a man about to get married."

"And so I am. And your litnany spoken like a woman in need of a compliment."

She chuckled, a little guilty at her use of deception to gain a compliment. "And so I am."

He pulled her into his arms and kissed her deeply.

When they broke apart, she stood there for a moment with her eyes closed and a smile curving her lips while she caught her breath and her pulse raced. Never had she had such a reaction as she did to Jason's kisses.

"Why do you smile?"

"Because each time you kiss me, I feel like I'm flying, being carried away on a wonderful sandalwood breeze."

"Are you disappointed when you find out it's only a kiss?"

"Never. It's not only a kiss, not to me. Besides, I know there will be more kisses to come, how can I be disappointed?"

He laughed.

"You're right about that, and there are many, many more kisses to come in our life together."

"You should take me home now before we do something we regret."

"I will never regret being with you, but I will wait until our wedding night to do so. We will consummate our vows then."

She nodded, snaked her hand around his neck and brought him down for a kiss.

"Yes, then. It's only a few days away, and then I'm yours for always."

"Always."

"There is something we should have discussed before I said yes. I want lots of children, Jason."

"No. No children. You might die."

"I won't die. I'm not Cassie. I'm strong. I'm like my mother, and she had twelve children. No one in my family has died in childbirth for as long as I can remember."

"No. Ways exist to protect you, and I

will use them."

How can he do this to me? I love him so much but no children. Why can't he understand I'm not Cassie? Does she have to cast a shadow over everything?

Rachel held back her tears. "I don't like it, but I don't know what I can do about it, but I insist that the first night you use nothing or do nothing to prevent my getting pregnant. I want our first time together to be real, totally without the hindrance of your methods to protect me. You must give me one opportunity to have a child."

Jason was quiet for a moment.

"Very well. Cassie didn't get pregnant for four years."

"See, it sounds like I don't have a chance in Hell, pardon my language, that I'll get pregnant, but I want that chance."

"All right you'll get your chance. Just once."

Rachel smiled and prayed that once would be all it took. If he saw that she was strong and wouldn't die in childbirth, he'd be more willing to have more children. Coming from a large family, she was sure he wanted more than two children.

"Hopefully, just once is all I'll need. My

mother was a very fertile woman, and I hope I take after her. I have eleven brothers and sisters. I want lots of kids."

"Twelve of you! Where are you in the pecking order?"

"I'm a middle child. I have three sisters older and three younger and two older brothers and three younger. Two of my older sisters and both of my older brothers are married and have children. Between the four of them, my mother has nineteen grandchildren. I'd like to add to that number. Besides, do you want Billy to be the only one responsible for us in our old age?" She shook her head. "No, of course, you don't. He needs siblings. If I only get to have one shot at having a child, I hope I have triplets."

He pushed away from her but held her at arm's length. "Good Lord, why would you wish that upon us?"

She cocked her head. How could he not understand? "So I can have as many children as possible from my only chance."

He threw up his arms. "All right, I give up. You'll have your chance. Just once. I don't want to lose you, too."

Rachel closed the gap between them.

She understood how hard this was for him and was thankful for the chance she was being given.

"Thank you. Thank you. Thank you." She kissed him all over his face. Little butterfly kisses, ending with a deep kiss on his lips before she pulled away and started down the path again.

Jason seemed thunder-struck and just stood there.

"Come on, or it'll be daylight before you get me home and we'll have way too many people to explain to."

He stared at her, then blinked furiously.

"What? Yes. Coming."

He quickly caught up with her and took her hand in his.

"You are an amazing woman. I had determined I would never have children and yet now you've convinced me that we should try at least once. Who would have thought such a thing would happen. Certainly not Al Pope."

She furrowed her eyebrows. "What does Alfred Pope have to do with anything?"

"He always bets against me.

"In this instance, too? I think this is something we should keep between ourselves."

"You're correct. I'm just generalizing. Al figures if he doesn't, no one will. He keeps me on my toes."

They took the buggy and reached the dormitory. Even though the temperature was chilly, Rachel wasn't ready for the night to end.

"Would you like to sit for a while?"

"Sure."

She led him up the steps to one of the porch swings.

"I'm so glad your men thought to put these on the porches. The ladies like to sit out here and watch the men go by. The event is almost like they are on parade. Waiting for one of us to choose them and bring them up to the swing. When all eight swings are full, the men disappear. It's rather strange."

"Not really. Each one of those men wants to get married. They figure by putting on their Sunday-go-to-meeting clothes and cleaning up, they have their best chance of snagging the attention of one of you ladies."

"Not me. You snagged my attention the first time I saw you standing behind the podium at the church and again when you stood on the ships wheel deck, legs apart and hands on your hips like the whole world was yours. I wondered what it would be like to have that much attention paid to me."

"And now?"

She looked up at the stars.

"Now I'm glad I didn't wait for you to find me. We might never have gotten together."

He held her hand as they sat, cocking his head to the side. "And you understand why."

"Yes, I do. Moving forward is very hard when you've lost someone you love. I know." She paused and took a deep breath. "Jason, I never told you, but I was engaged before. My fiancé enlisted in the Union Army two weeks before our wedding was to take place. He told me to wait. That he had to go because all of his forebears had served in the military."

He rubbed his thumb over the top of her hand as he held it. "He couldn't wait a few weeks, until after you were married?"

She didn't look at Jason but stared out over the street toward the ocean. "Ezra thought it was better that way, just in case he didn't come home. He died almost immediately. They sent him to Maryland the first of September. The seventeenth of

September he was dead. The battle was Antietam. I won't ever forget because I thought I died then, too.

"He wasn't even supposed to be in a battle. He was supposed to be a doctor. He'd completed his education but had not gone through the graduation ceremony yet. The army didn't care. They needed doctors."

Jason rubbed her hand gently and said quietly. "Then he was right wasn't he?"

She turned toward him, tears in her eyes. "No, he was wrong. If we'd married, I could have had a child to love when he was gone. As it was, I had nothing. Nothing but a memory."

He frowned, his eyebrows furrowed. "I'm sorry, Rachel. Sorry you had to go through that."

She leaned against his shoulder. "I'm not. Everything I've gone through brought me here to Seattle and you."

"I'm glad you feel that way."

She heard a husky tone to his voice. "So am I. Now kiss me and let me go inside. I intend to dream of you tonight."

He kissed her deeply and long. Tasting her and she him. Breathing hard they parted.

"Goodnight, my love."

"Goodnight, Rachel."

She went inside, a lot sadder than she thought she would be. The evening had been wonderful but Jason still refused to admit that he loved her. What if he never did? Was she prepared for that contingency?

Rachel took off her coat and hung it on one of the pegs on the wall by the door to her bedroom. She would not think about Jason now. They were getting married, and that is what she wanted, wasn't it?

CHAPTER 7

May 6, 1865

The day of the wedding was upon them. Lucy ran around like a chicken with its head cut off.

"I know we're forgetting something."

"Lucy. Please. Sit down and calm yourself. You're making me more nervous than anything else."

"Oh, Rach, I'm sorry. I just want everything to be perfect for you and Jason. You're my best friend. I don't want you to end up like my cousin Enid. Her wedding almost didn't happen. Her dress was ruined in the rain, and she stepped on the skirt, ripped the hem and about two feet of the skirt off. The wedding was a disaster. I want yours to be wonderful."

"It will be. Don't worry. As long as Jason and I are married by the end of the day, I'll be downright tickled."

Lucy looked lovely in her vibrant purple

dress. Her black hair and green eyes seemed even more vibrant than usual.

Rachel wore her grandmother's wedding dress. The garment was the last she was able to fit in her trunk. She'd taken out some of her linens to get all her dresses into the luggage.

The dress was completely out of style with cuffs about eight inches long with pearl buttons up them. Above the cuff, the sleeve puffed out a bit. The sweetheart neckline was cut low enough to show some cleavage and edged with the same pearls as on the buttons. The dress fell from an empire waist straight down to her ankles. There was an overskirt that opened down the front and also edged with the same pearls.

Rachel had loved this dress since she was a little girl. Her mother had worn the dress and had a beautiful marriage that was still going strong after almost forty years. Her grandmother's marriage lasted for thirty years until grandpa died while plowing the north forty acres.

The plow had gotten stuck, and he was attempting to dislodge it when suddenly the chain on the plow broke, hitting him in the head. The wound didn't kill him right away.

Grandma found him, saw the injury was too severe for a doctor to be of any help and stayed there in the field with him until he was gone. Then she got her sons to bring the body into the house where she prepared him for burial.

What an odd thing to think about on my wedding day. Wearing Grandma's dress must be making me dredge up memories showing me how amazing a woman Grandma was. I wish I had her locket.

Her grandmother was a strong woman who loved fiercely. She preferred to work the farm herself rather than marry some man to work it for her. The only man she'd ever let into her bed was gone, and she wasn't about to let anyone else in. She had seven sons and three daughters to help her, and she lived out her life in relative comfort on the farm.

Rachel agreed with her grandmother. Jason was the only man she wanted to marry. He represented everything she wanted in a husband. He was financially secure, physically strong so he could protect her and handsome. If for some unseen reason their marriage didn't happen, she would just never marry. But the wedding was happening. In less than an hour she would be Mrs. Jason Talbot. Rachel Emmaline Talbot.

"Are you ready?" Lucy asked from the door to Rachel's bedroom. Starting tonight, Lucy would serve as the 'head' of the brides here.

Butterflies filled her stomach, fluttering to and fro. "Yes, I'm ready."

Lucy laughed.

"Clancy is ready to give you away, and the sooner, the better says he."

"All right, let's go and put the poor man out of his misery."

Rachel took Lucy by the arm, hooking their elbows together, and walked out the door. Outside all the brides formed two lines with enough room for Rachel, followed by Lucy, to walk between them. Hers was the first of what Rachel hoped was many weddings to come. The lines extended from the dormitory to the church. Each woman greeted Rachel and gave her a flower. Gardenia, lily of the valley, lilac, tulips and violets were all in season. By the time she reached the church, Rachel had an enormous bouquet. So big she couldn't hold it. She pulled out two tulips and left the rest to the side of the steps up to the church door.

She entered the church and took Clancy's arm. Everyone whispered as they passed. He walked with her up to the front of the church where Jason waited. Rachel was thrilled he wasn't wearing his buckskins, but a three-piece suit, white shirt, and string tie. The white shirt emphasized the tan of his skin, and he looked so handsome, she almost swooned.

Reverend Peabody cleared his throat.

"Now children, settle down so we can get these two married."

He smiled first at Rachel and then at Jason.

"Dearly beloved, we are gathered together this day to marry this man to this woman. Do you Jason Christopher Talbot, take this woman Rachel Emmaline Sawyer to be your lawful wedded wife, to have and to hold through sickness and health, for richer or for poorer and to keep yourself only unto her for as long as you both shall live?"

"I do."

Jason's voice was so strong and when he looked over at her, he smiled and winked.

She lowered her head trying not to faint.

She wanted to yell from the rafters, but that would be unladylike.

Reverend Peabody continued.

"Do you Rachel Emmaline Sawyer promise to have and to hold through sickness and health, for richer or for poorer, to love and obey and to keep yourself only unto him for as long as you both shall live?"

"I do." Her voice wasn't nearly as strong as Jason's had been, but that didn't matter. She'd made her promise.

"By the power vested in me by Washington Territory and the City of Seattle, I pronounce you man and wife. You may kiss the bride."

Jason grinned.

Rachel raised her face for him to kiss.

He gathered her into his arms and held her close, then lowered his head and took her lips in the most amazing kiss he'd ever given her. He tantalized and teased, tasted and was tasted, explored her as never before and invited her to do the same. The kiss was one she felt all the way to her toes.

He broke the kiss, but when she looked up his grin was still there.

"Hello, Mrs. Talbot."

Heart pounding, she smiled back.

"Hello, Mr. Talbot."

"Shall we get this shindig started so we can get on the road to Olympia?"

She nodded.

"I need to change my dress. This one is not for dancing or riding in a wagon."

"Do you need a maid?"

"I could use some help. I'll get Lucy."

"No need. I'll help you."

They walked back to the dormitory and into her room.

"I've never had a man in here before. Men aren't usually allowed in the dormitories."

"I should hope not. Turn around, and I'll undo those little buttons."

She dutifully gave him her back. His deft fingers made short work of the tiny, intricate pearl buttons.

Rachel slipped the dress off her shoulders and let it pool on the floor before stepping out of it and folding it carefully and putting it back into her trunk. Then she took her purple dress and pulled it over her head.

"If we weren't going back, I might just have you stay in your corset and stockings."

"You are a very naughty man."

"Where my wife is concerned, I

certainly am."

Jason helped her, pulling the dress down over her ample bosom. She began to button the dress, but Jason shooed her hands away and took over the task himself.

He waggled his eyebrows.

"I must practice getting you into the dress in order to get you out of it later."

Rachel giggled.

"You're incorrigible."

"But, of course, *Madame* Talbot," he said with a French accent. "Now that you're dressed appropriately, *Madame*, shall we greet our friends?"

"But, of course, *Monsieur*."

His eyebrows furrowed, he gazed at her. "Rach, before we go back. Are you sure you want to leave today for Olympia? We could stay at the inn for our first night."

"No. I want to get to Olympia as quickly as possible, and with the wagon, it will take us longer, so I want to leave fairly early from the reception."

He lifted his brows and gave a slight shake of his head. "All right. Your wish is my command."

She grinned. "As it should be."

They walked outside and over to Dolly's

Saloon where the festivities were taking place. Music played, and the tables had been moved to the sides of the room, so the middle of the floor was available for dancing.

As they entered, the brides greeted them and hugged Rachel, the men came forward and shook Jason's hand.

Adam clapped him on the back. "Congratulations. You lucky dog."

Jason grinned each time someone congratulated him.

Every man there wanted to kiss her, even Alfred Pope. Rachel got more kisses on her cheek than she ever had in her life.

Alfred leaned down and bussed her cheek lightly. "I never thought I'd see the day that Jason Talbot married."

Rachel smiled. "Today's the day, Mr. Pope."

"When will you start calling me Al like everyone else?"

"Are you sure you want me to? That might mean we're friends."

"We are friends. Just because you had the poor taste to marry Jason instead of me, doesn't mean we're not friends."

"Very well. Al it is."

"Good. Now may I have this dance?"

Jason placed his hand on Rachel's shoulder. "Sorry old man, I'm stealing my bride. We have to get on the road if we're to reach a good place to camp for tonight."

Adam put his arm around Jason's shoulders. "Are you sure you don't want to stay at the inn for your first night?"

Jason shook his head. "We already talked about it. We'll camp tonight then stay in Olympia for the next two days, before coming home."

Adam frowned. "But Jason, your first night together shouldn't be on the ground or in a wagon. It should be in a nice soft bed."

Jason shrugged. "I know, and I agree, but Rachel insisted we head out to Olympia right after the wedding."

"That's because she hasn't any idea what a wedding night is supposed to be, but you do. You should be adamant."

He shook his head. "I'm not starting this marriage by becoming a tyrant and insisting on anything. I'll just do my best to make it easy for her. I will take care of my new bride. Trust me."

*****

The time was about three in the

afternoon when Jason helped Rachel into the wagon. He'd spread a folded blanket across the bench to make it a little more comfortable.

He climbed in beside her.

"Giddy up." She watched him slap the reins on the horses' butts to get them moving.

"Thank you." Rachel placed her arm around his and leaned against him.

"For what?"

"For the blanket. I know the trip will be a long one and this will help make it easier."

"Anything for my bride."

Rachel smiled.

They'd been traveling for a little more than four hours when Jason pulled off the main road and came to a stop. He jogged around to her side and helped her to the ground.

She was sore, and her buttocks screamed with pain. Rubbing them seemed to help a little.

"We'll make camp here and sleep in the wagon tonight."

"Why? Won't that be terribly cold?" Just the thought of the cold wagon bed made her shiver.

"Yes." Jason patted her arm. "Don't worry. I'll keep you warm." He waggled his eyebrows.

"Oh." She turned her head away, lest he see her blush. As hard as it had been to be forward and to pursue him, she was still the same girl who was uncomfortable with the intimacies of being married.

He chuckled. Then he gently turned her head with a knuckle to her chin. "Don't be embarrassed. Remember as husband and wife, we can talk about everything and say anything to each other."

Rachel lowered her gaze and smiled. "I'll try to remember that, but I'll probably still blush."

Jason laughed. "All right. Blush. Just don't forget to talk to me if something bothers you. Anything."

She nodded. "I won't."

Rachel couldn't help but wonder what her wedding night would be like. She really wasn't thrilled about disrobing out here in the wild to put on her nightgown, but if Jason wanted her to, she supposed she would. She looked skyward. "Jason, I know this is our wedding night, but you said I could tell you anything. Well, I don't want to have to undress tonight. It's cold, and I just don't feel comfortable getting naked, even to put on a nightgown."

"I understand, and it's all right we don't need to consummate our vows tonight. I'd rather have a real bed for your first time and have us both be more comfortable and relaxed. Don't think about it any longer."

Jason made a fire and Rachel fixed coffee while Jason prepared their bed in the wagon. Adam had packed them a picnic of sandwiches. She didn't know what kind of meat, but she thought probably beef and could even have been bear, and she wouldn't have minded, now that she'd eaten the meat before. He'd also included apples, two quarts of stew, cheese, cookies, dishes, utensils and a bottle of wine.

She looked over the food before she set all the tasty offerings. "My word, Adam has made us a veritable feast."

"Good. The food will be our breakfast, too."

When the coffee finished boiling, Rachel spread a blanket on the ground and set the food on it. She handed Jason a plate and cutlery as well as a cup of coffee.

"I thought we might hold off on the wine

until we are in the hotel in Olympia." Jason took a bite of sandwich. "Mmm. Roast beef and cheese with butter. Adam will make some woman a fine wife someday."

Rachel laughed.

"Don't you dare tell him I said that."

She cocked an eyebrow. "What will you give me to keep your secret?"

"This." He leaned over and kissed her.

"Well, that will do for a start."

"Sassy woman. I'm seeing a different side of the sweet, naïve girl I thought I married."

"Now that I have you, I can be my ornery self…sometimes."

"Yes, my dear, you can. Never be afraid to be who you are when you're with me."

He looked down into his coffee cup.

"Rachel, about tonight. Even though we won't consummate our marriage vows tonight, you're my wife and tonight I get to hold you in my arms. That's enough for now."

She let out a huge sigh. "I look forward to being held by you all night."

"Well, as I said, don't even think about it. Let's sit by the fire with our coffee and cookies."

"I'd like that."

She picked up the blanket and spread it on the log and the ground in front of it.

Jason sat on the blanket with the log at his back and patted the space next to him.

She gathered her skirt close, handed him her coffee cup and settled on the blanket next to him. "This poor blanket will never come clean."

"It doesn't have to. It stays in the wagon for times such as these.'

He put his arm around her shoulders and brought her close.

"This is nice."

She leaned her head on his chest.

"It is. You know I think even more stars are visible here than at your home."

"It's your home now, too."

"I'll have to remember that."

"Remembering will be easier once you're actually living there."

"I suppose so. I can't wait to have my own home. To live there and start our family there."

They were quiet for a bit, drinking their coffee and eating their cookies.

Jason broke the silence. "I think I'm ready for bed."

"Are you tired already?"

He shook his head. "Not really, but I'm ready to have you in my arms and kiss you and think about making love to you. Tonight will be a difficult night for me. I want you so badly I can hardly stand it."

Thrilled that he desired her, she placed her hand on his leg. "We could...you know...if you really want to."

He leaned down and kissed her gently. "No, my sweet wife. I'm a man. I can control my urges. We will wait."

Rachel grew up on a farm. She heaved a sigh of relief that they would not be coupling tonight. Knowing what was expected of her and knowing pain was involved, she didn't mind waiting.

Jason helped her up into the wagon where he'd prepared their bed for the night.

Rachel took off her coat and crawled under the blankets. The covers were as cold or colder than she was and made her shiver even more.

By the time Jason got in beside her, she shook with cold.

"Come here, sweetheart."

He stretched out an arm.

Gratefully, she pressed her body against

the warmth of his. Then he wrapped his arm around her and covered them both with the blankets.

Slowly, she warmed and relaxed into his body. She looked forward to doing this for the rest of her life. Rachel liked the feeling of being safe, warm, protected and desired.

Now there was just one problem...she had another day to worry about her wedding night.

CHAPTER 8

The next day they pulled into Olympia around three. Jason had hustled them onto the road early, leaving their campsite around seven o'clock according to her pin watch.

He stopped the wagon in front of the *Grand Hotel*.

The large pale yellow three-story building looked well maintained, and Rachel was ready to get off the wagon for a while. Even though Jason had stopped every couple of hours so they could stretch, her bum was none too happy with the hard seat, and neither was her back. She thought she'd get used to the lack of comfort when they traveled, but this time the trip was painful.

After Jason helped her down, she walked around in a circle, stretching her legs.

"I'm so looking forward to sleeping in a real bed tonight."

"I know the bed wasn't the most comfortable, but you'll be glad of the wagon bed when we head back. We'll have to sleep on the ground then."

She stopped walking in front of him. "Don't remind me. Do you suppose the hotel has a bathing room?"

He shrugged. "I don't know. I've never actually stayed here before, but we can certainly ask."

"Oh, where do you stay when you come?"

Carrying their valises, Jason followed her up the steps to the hotel. "Usually with the wagon at the stable since it's just one night if any. Most of the time we come in get our supplies and leave for home again the same day."

"Well, I'm glad we're staying here for a few days. I'm not looking forward to our return trip."

"When we go home, I'll make an effort to keep you warm, and we'll use our coats as blankets, too. We'll be cozy. I promise."

Rachel enjoyed his caring attitude toward her and the effort he was making to see she was comfortable. She looked him up and down then cocked her head to the side. "I suppose I trust you. But for right now, let's get checked in and see about a bath."

Entering the lobby from the boardwalk

was like entering an entirely different world. The lobby was decorated in vibrant blues. The Oriental carpet in front of the desk held a beautiful starry design in midnight blue. The floor was wood, oak maybe, she didn't know, but it was polished to a high sheen. To her right, a sofa and single Queen Anne chair, both covered in light blue damask, formed a conversation area in front of the window.

To her left was a restaurant, and lovely smells emanated through the door into the lobby where they stood.

"Mmm. Something smells good." She closed her eyes and sniffed.

The young red-haired woman behind the counter smiled. "That would be today's special roast beef dinner. Cook is from England and always makes a Yorkshire pudding to go with the roast. A favorite meal around here, so if you want some, I recommend getting seated as soon as possible."

Rachel looked up at Jason. "We missed lunch today so I am rather hungry. How about you?"

He nodded. "Yeah, me, too. Just as soon as we get a room key from this young lady, we'll go eat."

"Yes, sir. I'm Jessie, and I'd be happy to check you in. Do you have reservations?"

"Yes. I mailed a letter requesting a room for three nights. Jason Talbot is the name."

She looked down at the desk, then back at them, smiling.

"I understand this is your wedding trip. We've set aside our best room. It has a bathing room, and I can send up men with hot and cold water if you would like a bath right away."

Her stomach growled, and Rachel pressed a hand to her middle to squelch the sound.

"I think we should eat first and then have the bath."

Jason laughed. "Very well. We'll eat after we take the bags to the room."

"If you'll just sign the register here," the girl pointed at the next vacant line on the sheet. "The room is 108 and is down at the end of this hallway."

Jason signed the register, and the clerk handed him the key which he pocketed. Then he picked up the luggage and ducked his head toward Rachel. "My lady. I follow you."

Rachel giggled and headed down the hall.

Jason opened the door and set the bags inside without even going in the room. "We can check the accommodations out when we return, but I'm hungry now."

"So am I."

They walked back up the hall and crossed the lobby into the restaurant where they were seated in the middle of the room, away from the windows. They took the girls advice and placed their order for a meal of roast beef, Yorkshire pudding, roasted potatoes, peas, fresh bread, and butter. They finished off the meal with a slice of cherry pie.

Jason took her hand as it rested on the table.

"Are you ready for your bath? I promise to scrub your back if you scrub mine."

Rachel's mouth fell open and then she glanced around to see if anyone heard him. "Are you proposing what I think you are?"

Jason winked. "Probably. What do you think I'm proposing?"

She leaned forward and whispered. "That we bathe together…at the same time…in the same tub."

Jason chuckled. "Yes, my dear. That is what I'm suggesting. We'll get clean together, and hopefully, you'll relax some as you get used to us being without clothes in front of each other."

Rachel's heart beat wildly. She didn't know whether to be mortified or intrigued. She decided on intrigued.

"Very well, let's get the water sent to the room."

They stopped at the front desk, ordered the water and then headed down to room 108.

The room was lovely. Rachel walked the perimeter, running her fingers along the furnishings. A double canopy bed, covered with a wedding ring quilt, dominated the room, flanked by end tables that matched the posts on the canopy which were a light wood, maybe oak or maple. Also in the room were a six-drawer bureau and a tall boy dresser. A door on the wall directly opposite the bed led to the bathing room.

The large, claw-footed bathtub took up nearly the entire room. A pot-bellied stove provided heat and kept the water in one of the buckets warm for rinsing off the soap.

After the water arrived and Jason tipped

the men who brought it, Rachel gave him her back as she unbuttoned her bodice and let the dress drop in a pool of cotton around her.

"You can turn around. I like to watch you undress."

"You do? I thought the end result was what you were interested in."

Jason walked over and took her hands in his.

"I'm interested in all of it, you undressing and redressing is part of the enjoyment. My undressing should please you as well."

Rachel swallowed hard. She stood there in her corset and petticoats having a conversation with her husband like nothing was supposed to be embarrassing. He held her hands and smiled, doing his best to keep her at ease. And she was. Jason looked at her face, not her body. He wasn't in any hurry but was more concerned with her comfort.

"Well, if you undressing is supposed to bring me pleasure then hadn't you better get started."

Jason laughed. "That's my saucy wife."

He pulled his buckskin shirt over his

head. Under that, he wore a short-sleeved cotton undershirt.

She guessed that garment was to keep him comfortable when the buckskin got hot. Then he pulled off the undershirt and her breathing stopped. Jason was splendid to look upon. Even though it was only May, his skin tanned from working in the sun and his muscles rippled across his broad chest with every movement he made. If Rachel had been the swooning type, she'd have fainted dead away at the sight of her husband.

Pulse racing, she moved forward and placed her hand on his chest, feeling the sprinkling of curly brown hair. The curls wrapped around her questing fingers as if to trap them and hold them there forever.

"You're glorious. I never knew a man could appear as you do, so muscular and tan and…amazing to look at as you are."

He grinned. "Spoken like a true wife."

Jason reached forward and opened the top hook on her corset. "You're behind, my lovely. Let me help you catch up."

In no time flat, he had her corset open and headed for the floor to form a pile on top of her dress. Her petticoat, chemise, and bloomers soon added to the collection on the floor.

"You're behind again." She bent over to roll her stockings down her legs. Soon, her heartbeat pounded in her chest, and she was naked, in body and emotionally.

In a minute or two Jason had followed her, and they both stood looking at each other, examining each curve, every dimple and more.

"You're beautiful," he said after a few minutes passed.

Sure she was pink from head to toe at being looked at so frankly, she had to stop covering herself with her arms. She looked him up and down, stopping her perusal at his member. He was big perhaps too large.

He chuckled.

Her gaze popped up to his.

He winked at her.

"I'd say the same to you, but you're magnificent."

"Thank you my lovely." He walked forward a few steps and put his hands on her shoulders, lightly kissed her lips before scooping her up and carrying her to the bathing chamber.

He set her on the floor next to the tub where the steam wafted into the air.

She bent over and tested it.

"The water is good and hot, but not too hot. It will relax us and our muscles."

Rachel climbed in the tub and placed her back against one end.

Jason sat against the other.

She stretched her legs between his and couldn't touch his member, though she could definitely see it. Jason was ready, willing and able to have relations with her.

She soaped her body with her rose soap and rinsed before standing and turning her back to Jason before sitting again.

He washed her back with a washcloth and then just his hands. They came around and cupped her breasts, tweaked her nipples with his fingers.

The intimate touch sent shockwaves through her woman's center.

Her head fell back against his chest. "Jason." She breathed the word, having almost lost the capability to speak. "What are you doing to me?"

"I'm making love to you. The final act is just the beginning. You'll see. Do you like what I'm doing?"

"Yes." Her eyes closed. "Very much."

He ran his hands over her belly and

down toward her mons, but he didn't touch her there.

Suddenly he stood, grabbed bucket of warm, clear water and poured half of the bucket over his head.

"Stand please."

Rachel rose, and he poured the rest of the water over her rinsing the soap from her.

Then he reached into the tub and lifted Rachel out, pressed her wet body against his and let her slide all the way down.

He took a clean towel and dried every square inch of her. She figured he would be in a hurry, but he took his time.

When she was finally dry, he dried himself before lifting her in his arms and carrying her to the bed.

"If I do anything that you don't like or that frightens you, let me know. Having relations should be a pleasant undertaking. I admit this first time won't be completely pain-free for you, but I'll do my best to give you pleasure first. Will you trust me?"

She looked him in the eyes, all too aware of her breasts resting on his chest. His blue orbs stared back at her and without any deceit in them, nothing but caring. "Yes. I trust you."

"Good. Let's lie on the bed and get to know each other a bit."

Unsure of his meaning, she sat, scooted to the middle of the bed and then lay down.

Jason came down beside her and propped himself up on one bent arm while the fingers of his other hand, skittered over her body, lightly touching and then moving to another place, making her entire being come alive with want.

She closed her eyes, unable to keep them open while such pleasure coursed through her flesh from the magic of his finger-tips.

"Oh, Jason." She breathed out his name. Her heart pounded in her chest, and she was sure he could hear it, but she had no control, not over her heart-beat or her breathing or anything else at the moment.

"Like that do you, sweetheart?"

"Oh, yes." Her voice quivered of its own accord. She sounded like a school girl, not a full-grown woman, but she'd never felt anything like this before.

His fingers circled her breasts and captured her nipple with his fingers, squeezing it just a little before his mouth closed over it.

At the touch of his tongue, she arched

off the bed. Then she grabbed Jason by the hair and shoved her nipple farther into his mouth. Rachel couldn't get enough, couldn't get close enough, or feel enough to satisfy her. She wanted so much more.

Then he let go of her breast and kissed her stomach again and again as he worked his way downward. Before she knew what was to happen, he put his mouth there, below her mons and pleasured her as she shattered into a million shining stars. She wanted to scream with the pleasure but doubted she had.

"You're a noisy little thing. I must remember that when we are home. Can't have you shrieking every time I give you satisfaction."

Breathless, she found it difficult to speak. "I screamed? I thought that was someone else."

He chuckled. "No, my dear that was you."

"Oh, my." She turned away her face.

With a knuckle, he turned it back. "Don't turn away from me when I give you pleasure. Being able to enjoy being together in all ways is a wonderful part of marriage."

"You're not embarrassed by me...by my

yelling."

"Not in the least. I'm thrilled that you have such a reaction, although we will have to figure out a way to stifle that when we are at home. My brothers will understand, but Billy will think I'm killing you."

She grinned. "We can't have that. I'd be mortified if he asked me if I was all right."

"To say nothing of the ribbing I would get from my brothers. Now if you are feeling good, another part of our having relations is to come. Still trust me?"

"Yes." She stiffened, her nerves getting the best of her.

Jason rose over her and covered her with his body. She felt some pressure and a little pain, but nothing horrible as he made love to her. This action was the part where the babies were created and she hoped against hope she would prove to be as fertile as her mother.

Later, after they were both replete, she lay cuddled up to Jason's side, her leg flung over his and his arm around her. She played with his chest hair, unable to resist the silky soft curls.

"What do we do now?"

"Well, if the time were later, we'd go to

sleep. If it were any other but your first time making love, we would do that again and again, but you are tender now." He slowly rubbed her shoulder, relaxing her. "So I suggest that we dress and take in the sights of the big city of Olympia. Didn't you want to do some shopping while we're here?"

"I want to buy material for new dresses for me and shirts for you, your brothers and Billy. I also want to see if the mercantile has a sewing machine. With that new clothes wouldn't take any time at all." Her hand stopped and was still upon his chest. "A machine is kind of expensive though."

"How much are they?"

"Around seventy-five dollars."

He whistled. "That is pricey."

"It's all right. I shouldn't have asked. I can sew the garments by hand."

He put his hand on his chin and furrowed his brows. "No. You should ask for whatever you want and need. If you can sew our clothes with this machine, that will save us a lot of money down the road. My brothers and I are big men, and the readymade shirts and pants don't fit us well. You sewing our clothes would be very efficient." He nodded. "I think we should get you a machine. Let's see if we can find one."

Rachel leaned up and kissed her husband's cheek. "You're the best husband ever."

He lifted an eyebrow. "Just remember you said that when I disagree with you."

"Other than about the children, what makes you think you'll disagree with me?"

"How about the mystery you're trying to solve? I disagree with you about that, and I'll keep doing so until you let the sheriff take care of it."

Rachel smiled and batted her eyes. "I could get used to your teasing, but I know you love me, so you'll do anything for me."

Jason was immediately quiet but continued to rub her back with his hand. Finally, he said, "We'll see."

She knew as soon as the words were out of her mouth that she shouldn't have said them. They hadn't mentioned love...ever. Just because she'd fallen in love with him didn't mean he loved her, as well. Rachel wasn't stupid. She knew Jason had loved Cassie and was devastated when she died. But that happened almost ten years ago. Now was the time for him to let go of her and let Rachel fill her place…at least part of her place.

The moment was gone. Whatever had been happening between them had died. Rachel took a minute and put on a brave face.

"Well, shall we get dressed and see if you can find me a sewing machine?"

Jason straightened the arm he'd been holding her with so she could scoot away.

"Yes, I suppose we should. There is something else we need to discuss."

"What is that?"

"The thefts. This mystery you're determined to solve. I want you to let the sheriff do his job."

"I've come so far. I need to see this through. One of my two suspects is guilty."

Jason closed his eyes and pinched the skin between them.

"And you wondered what else we would disagree about."

They both stood and dressed.

"Are you ready?" Rachel turned toward him and found him watching her from the chair.

"Of course. You know you are lovely. Watching you dress is pleasurable and almost makes me forget our disagreement."

"I'm sorry we disagree, but let's not talk about that now. I want to enjoy our little honeymoon."

"You're right and seeing you now makes me want to grant you anything."

She grinned.

"But I won't. We'll talk later, my beautiful bride."

She looked down at the floor, knowing she blushed, but then gazed back at her husband. "Thank you. I like looking at you, too. You took my breath away the first time I saw you without a shirt."

Jason raised his eyebrows. "How many men have you seen without their shirts?"

She ducked her head a bit. "Just my father and brothers and I had no desire to touch them."

"Thank God, for that."

Realizing she misspoke, she shook her head. "You know what I mean."

Jason chuckled. "Yes, I do. Your father and brothers probably work in offices and don't need to use their muscles as I do."

"A couple of my brothers do, but most still farm, but even if they were as muscular as you, I only want to touch you."

He stood. "I'm glad. Now let's go before I find a reason to get you back in bed and my arms."

She shook her head. "You're insatiable."

"You have no idea. When you are not sore anymore, I'll give you an idea how voracious a lover I can be."

Rachel picked up her reticule. "You say the most outrageous things."

"Only the truth, my dear. Only the truth."

She opened the door. "Shall we go before you get any more *voracious* ideas?"

He laughed, closed the door and locked it before pocketing the key. Then he placed Rachel's hand in the crook of his elbow, and they walked out of the hotel.

As happy as she was, she wondered if Jason would ever love her as she did him. What if he didn't or couldn't? What then? Where did that leave her?

CHAPTER 9

They could have asked the clerk for directions to a mercantile, but this way was more fun. She liked exploring the stores in new towns, finding treasures she wouldn't have otherwise.

After going into several shops that carried ladies things, hats, clothes, material and so forth, they went into the hardware store.

Jason held open the door. "I need to pick up more axes."

Rachel was following him, through aisles filled with all kinds of tools for farming, ranching, and logging. She saw shovels, pitchforks, and plows, axes and saws, ropes and wire of various kinds. That's when she spotted it. To her right against the far wall was a sewing machine.

"Jason, look." She pointed at the piece of equipment and then hurried over to examine the machine. "It's perfect."

The device was a piece of furniture in its

own cabinet. The treadle on the bottom was fancy wrought iron with scrolls and swirls. Drawers for the thread, needles, bobbins, and scissors were on either side of the cabinet below the sewing machine, with room in the middle for the seamstress to put her knees.

Rachel fell in love at once.

"Can we get it, Jason? Please?"

He looked over the piece of machinery and talked to the store owner, a thin, balding man with a full beard who appeared to be about fifty.

"How much for the sewing machine?"

"One-hundred twenty-five dollars."

"I'll give you fifty," countered Jason.

The owner raised his eyebrows. "One-hundred."

Jason shook his head. "Seventy-five and that's my final offer."

The owner pulled the beard on his chin into a point. "Sold."

Jason looked down at her and winked, then grinned. "We'll be back to pick it up on Tuesday morning." He pulled an elaborate money clip made of what appeared to be sterling silver with gold accents out of his pocket. He peeled off seventy-five dollars and handed the bills to the proprietor of the hardware store, and returned the money clip to his pocket.

Rachel had never seen as much money in her life as Jason appeared to have in his money clip. And his negotiation with the owner of the store was quite impressive. She'd have to remember that for when the two of them might be in talks for something, like having children.

The owner counted the money and put it in his pocket. "That'll be fine, Mr...."

"Talbot, Jason Talbot."

"Okay Mr. Talbot, I'm Otto Meyer. I own this place. Can I do anything else for you?" The storekeeper took a small pad of paper and a pencil out of his apron pocket.

"Yes, I need twenty-five axes, five hundred feet of rope and six two-man saws." Jason used his fingers to count the items he wanted

The man scribbled on his pad. "I'm not sure I have that many axes in stock, but if not I'll get them and have them shipped to you. I should have everything else. Will you be picking up those with the sewing machine?"

Jason nodded. "Yes. Thank you. Where

is the best restaurant?"

"That'd be the Olympia Bakery and Café, just down the street. Everyone loves it because the baked goods are the best so go early. Otherwise, you'll have a good long wait." The storekeeper put the notepad and pencil back in his apron.

Jason looked down at Rachel. "Are you hungry now? It's almost five."

She nodded. "Oh yes, I could definitely eat."

Jason shifted his gaze to Mr. Meyer. "Is now too early?"

The man shook his head. "Absolutely not. It should be the perfect time. Betty will have just pulled the last loaves of bread from the oven. Her pork sandwiches are wonderful. You won't be sorry. Just turn right when you leave here. The café is about four blocks down. You can't miss it."

Jason extended his hand. "Thank you, Mr. Meyer. We'll take your advice, and we'll be back on Tuesday with the wagon for the goods."

Mr. Meyer shook Jason's hand. "I'll have everything prepared for travel by ten o'clock on Tuesday morning."

"Thank you, sir. You've helped my

husband make me a delighted woman today." Rachel bowed her head just a little in acknowledgment.

"Pleased to be of help, Mrs. Talbot," said the shopkeeper.

They left the hardware store and headed for the café.

Jason patted her hand where it rested on his arm. "You saved us fifty dollars today."

She slanted a look his way. "How did I do that? I never said a word."

"You told me how much sewing machines cost. If I hadn't known, I would have paid the one-hundred twenty-five that the owner was asking for the machine."

"Oh, well, in that case, we can get extra material. I can get started on Christmas shirts for your brothers."

"They'll be mighty grateful. So will I."

"But you wear buckskin. The needles are not strong enough to go through the leather."

"I don't always wear these. I didn't for our wedding."

"You're right you didn't. You wore a three-piece suit and looked marvelous. I'm surprised I remember much of the wedding other than the 'I do's'. The day went so fast."

He grinned and then winked. "Well, that's the most important thing to remember."

They went to the café and were seated immediately, though the table was in front of the windows.

Entering from the crisp air outside, she smelled the scent of yeasty bread and heard dozens of conversations going on. "Now I wish we'd come even earlier." Rachel pulled off her gloves.

"Why is that?" Jason picked up his fork and examined it.

"Because I hate sitting in front of the windows. I feel like I'm on display, but I don't see any other open tables."

Filling the room were square tables covered with red-and-white checked tablecloths. Most sat four people, but a few against the walls and those in front of the windows held only two.

A waitress arrived and handed them menus. "Our special today is beef stew served with fresh, hot bread and apple pie for dessert. Can I get you something to drink while you look at the menu?"

"Yes, please. I'd like a glass of water."

Rachel's throat was dry as dust. They hadn't had anything to drink since their meal just after two."

After the petite brown-haired girl left to get the drinks, Rachel said, "Mmm, that beef stew sounds good."

"You should order it then."

When she'd lived in New Bedford, eating out at a restaurant was an extraordinary treat, and when she'd lived on the farm, they never ate anywhere but at home. She wanted to make sure she was making the perfect decision. "But the man at the hardware store recommended the pork sandwiches."

"I'll get the sandwich, two actually, and you can order the stew. Then we'll each taste the other's dinner and see what we like better. We still have several more meals before we go home."

"That sounds like a wonderful idea. After looking at the menu, I see several other dishes that I'd like to try."

Their orders came, and the offerings devoured as though she and Jason were starving.

"I must have been hungrier than I thought. This meal was wonderful." Rachel dabbed her napkin at the corners of her mouth. "Do you think we could entice Betty, the baker, to move to Seattle?"

Jason shrugged. "I doubt it. Besides, we already have a bakery. Perhaps the bread isn't quite as tasty, but the cakes are great."

"I'll bet you my pies are the best you've ever had, and you'll want them instead of cake."

"That's rather boastful don't you think?"

She raised her chin a bit. "It's not boastful if it's true."

He cocked an eyebrow. "No, I don't suppose it is, but your pies will have to be something extraordinary to beat Mrs. Jones cakes."

"They are." She lifted her eyebrows and smiled. "Trust me."

"We'll have a family bake-off when we get back. Your pies against Mrs. Jones' cakes with the name of the winner never leaving our house."

She raised her shoulders and shook her head a couple of times. "Why?"

"Because if you bake better than she does, people will want you to bake for them and you'll have plenty of baking to do just for the Talbots."

"Ah, see," she pointed at him. "You do think my pies will win."

"Of course, I do. I wouldn't be a very loyal husband if I thought anything else now would I?"

"No, you wouldn't."

Jason paid the bill leaving a good tip for the waitress.

Rachel placed her hand in the crook of Jason's arm. "Where to now?"

"What else would you like to do?"

"Well...I..." She looked upward through her lashes. "I've had enough shopping for today. I find myself rather tired. How do you feel about an early evening?"

He slowed his pace, then stopped altogether and looked at her. "You know I can't have relations with you yet, don't you?"

She looked around to make sure no one could hear their conversation then lowered her chin and spoke softly. "Yes, but that doesn't mean you can't hold me in your arms while we rest. And we won't get this opportunity again for a long time."

"No, we won't. Shall we go *rest*, Mrs. Talbot?"

"I believe we shall, Mr. Talbot."

They set off for the hotel and Rachel had to run to keep up with Jason's long strides. Her husband was in as much of a hurry as she was.

When they reached the room, Rachel practically ripped open her bodice, the little buttons down the front of the blouse were difficult for her shaking hands to unfasten.

"Here, let me help." Jason stood in only his pants and unfastened her buttons faster than she could.

Once she was free, Rachel disrobed quicker than she ever had before, but she had so many more clothes than Jason did that he still beat her. She didn't turn her back on him this time. Instead, she locked eyes with him as he lay on the bed, legs crossed at the ankles and a big smile on his face.

She lay down next to her husband, he put his arm around her and covered them both with the blankets. Rachel didn't think she'd fall asleep. Sleeping next to Jason was still too new, and she was too conscious of their nakedness to relax.

When she awoke, she was cuddled into Jason's side.

"About time, sleepyhead."

His deep voice made his chest rumble as he spoke.

Unable to resist, she turned her head and kissed his chest.

"How long have you been awake?"

"Not that long. Just enough to watch you sleep a little while and hear you snore."

Aghast, her eyes widened. "I don't snore."

"Oh it's quiet, but snore…you definitely do."

She lifted her chin and tried to turn away.

He chuckled and tightened his arm.

"Come here." He lifted her chin with a finger and claimed her lips with his.

When they broke apart, he grinned. "That's a much better way to wake up. Kissing first thing upon waking is a definite must."

"I agree. Shall we dress?" Now she grinned. "We can walk the other side of the street and see how much more of your money I can spend."

Rachel enjoyed the two-day honeymoon in Olympia but too soon it was time to go home. The thought of sleeping in a house with six males was daunting. She came from a large family it was true, but she'd never been the only woman in the house.

As they drove out of town, a small dog limped across the road in front of them.

"Oh, Jason. Stop."

"What for?"

She pointed to the side of the road. "That dog needs help. Please. I can't stand to see it in such a state."

Jason pulled the wagon to a halt and jumped down to approach the dog.

"The dog is a female and, if I'm not mistaken, is about to give birth."

Rachel gripped the edge of the wagon seat and could see the dog was in a bad way.

At first, the animal cowered when Jason approached, but he put out his hand, let her sniff it and talked gently until she calmed down, allowing him to come near.

He picked her up in his arms and put her in the back of the wagon on a blanket behind the bench.

Jason looked over at Rachel. "Since it looks like she'll have a home with us, what are you going to name her?"

Rachel looked back at the poor, dark brown animal, with white socks and as she did, the dog started wagging her tail.

"I think I'll name her Lucky. She's fortunate that we came by when we did."

"She is that. Why don't you give her some of a roast beef sandwich we had Betty pack for us? She looks like she needs it more than I do."

Rachel leaned against the back of the seat. Her hands could just reach the top of the dogs head and Rachel pet the poor animal. "Of course. Why didn't I think of that? We'll have to get her some water, too. She looks like she needs both. If she weren't pregnant, the poor creature would be skin and bones."

"That's true. I could feel every one of the animal's ribs when I picked her up. She's a tiny thing, but she ought to weigh at least ten or fifteen pounds, and I bet she's not half that."

Rachel took a sandwich out of the basket. She leaned over and gave the dog less than a quarter of the sandwich. Lucky scarfed it down like she was starving, which Rachel supposed she was. She continued to give her small bites until she'd eaten just over half the sandwich. Lucky would have kept eating, but because the dog was so little, Rachel didn't want her to hurt herself by overeating.

When they stopped for the night, Jason lifted the dog and set her on the ground. She stood and looked up at Rachel, and she could almost see fear in the animal's eyes.

"Don't worry Lucky. We're not leaving you."

Rachel gave Lucky the other half of the sandwich and water from her dinner plate which was more like a pie tin.

The dog drank almost a full pan of water before she lay down and curled up next to Rachel.

Jason jutted his chin toward the dog. "I think Lucky has adopted you."

Rachel pet the dog's head. "Good, because I've taken a liking to her, too. When we get home will you build a box big enough for her and her puppies, please?"

"Where do you propose to put it after I've built it?"

"In the kitchen behind the stove. It'll be nice and warm there for Lucky and her family."

"You seem to have it all figured out."

"I've always wanted a dog. My father said, twelve children, all wanting a pet of their own would be too many animals, so no one got a pet." Lucky was another addition to make her family complete.

"Well, I can imagine how he must have felt, but I see no reason for you not to have Lucky. I'd say the dog deserves someone who will love her. She obviously hasn't had someone to protect her in her life."

Rachel reached over and petted the animal. She too felt her ribs.

"The first thing she gets when we return home is a bath. The poor thing has matted hair all over. By the time I get done cutting the knots out, she'll be practically bald."

Jason nodded. "But she'll be clean and on her way to being healthy. By the looks of her, she has a long way to go. I'd say she's been on her own for a long time."

"She seems content now. Lucky is resting and look…" she pointed at the dog's belly. "You can see the puppies move. I don't think it's going to be long before she gives birth. I just hope we make it home first."

"So do I. If she starts having puppies, you may have to help her unless you know how to drive the wagon."

She shrugged. "I grew up on a farm, so I know how to drive a wagon, but I can help her with the puppies, too. No problem. I've had to pull calves and lambs. Puppies will be easy. Besides that the wagon is so full of supplies, there's barely room behind the seat for the dog. It will be easier for me to maneuver to help her."

He lifted his brows. "Goodness. Who knew I married such a talented woman."

"I know how, but I'd rather not deliver puppies in a wagon. I hope she can wait until we get home."

Giving Lucky a home was an indication that my longtime wish for a family is coming true. Maybe that bodes well for my bigger want of Jason loving me. I hope so.

CHAPTER 10

Wednesday, May 10, 1865

Lucky started to whine and squirm.

Rachel looked down at the little dog. Her stomach stiffened for several seconds. She was in labor.

"She's having the puppies, Jason. Pull over."

"We're only about an hour from home. I'm staying on the road. No telling how long this labor could go on. When you see her start to deliver a pup, I'll pull over, but for now, stopping is not necessary."

I shouldn't have panicked. "You're right. This labor could last hours or just minutes."

Rachel kept glancing back at Lucky, but the dog still hadn't started to deliver by the time they reached Seattle.

They arrived in town and drove on through up the mountain to the Talbot home.

Jason pulled the wagon onto its flat parking space in front of the house and set the brake. When he got to Rachel's side, he reached up, took her by the waist and lifted her to the ground.

She was always amazed by his strength.

"Please bring Lucky into the house and help me set up a bed for her. I have a feeling she'll have her puppies before the night is out."

She watched the little dog, whose body wracked with labor pains.

"I wish I could do something to help her."

"Not a thing we can do except try and make her comfortable. When the puppies come, they come. She's so small I can't imagine she'll have more than two or three pups." He frowned and furrowed his brows. "I don't think she can handle more than that. I have a box in the barn that will work as a bed. We'll just use the blanket she's on and put it in the box."

Rachel watched Jason and wondered if his frown meant he was thinking about Cassie and her dying.

"I agree, though I've seen dogs her size have five or six puppies. Then, having enough milk for all of them is difficult for the mom. Usually, a couple of the pups die."

"We'll just wait and see."

"Will you get the box now, please?" She looked around. "Where are all your brothers and Billy? The house is quiet."

"The brothers are at work, and Billy is probably fishing with his friend Leroy. I think we have the house to ourselves." He waggled his eyebrows. "Shall we take advantage of the privacy after we get Lucky settled?"

I love making love with Jason and even though he doesn't call it making love, that is what I think of it as.

"What about the wagon? It needs to be unloaded."

He took her hand. "The wagon can wait."

Jason first took her to the barn, and he retrieved the box, which he placed on the floor behind the stove.

Rachel folded the blanket and laid the wool blanket in the box while Jason held the dog. When they were sure Lucky was comfortable, Jason took Rachel to his bedroom, now their bedroom. He walked to the bed and then unfastened the buttons on her dress, getting the garment off her in record time.

While he shed his clothes, she finished with hers and then lay on the bed.

He stood and looked down at her.

She held up her arms to him and welcomed him to her.

They made love, Rachel refused to think of the act as having relations. She thought this time was perhaps sweeter than the first time. Maybe because she felt no pain only pleasure.

"Dad."

Billy's voice sounded from downstairs.

Jason cursed, walked across the room, shut the door and locked it. Then he came back, kissed her soundly and dressed in a hurry.

As quickly as she could, she did the same.

When both of them were presentable, Jason unlocked the door, and they went down to greet *their* son.

"Billy. I didn't expect you home for quite a while." Jason pointed at the string of fish his son held. "I know what we're having for dinner. Those look like really nice ones."

"Rachel patted her hair to make sure all

of the blonde curls were in place, and nothing was hanging. "That's an amazing mess of fish you have there." At least twenty fish were on the line. So many the boy could hardly hold them off the ground. Scales covered his plaid shirt from carrying them home. From the looks of his garment, he'd carried them over his shoulder.

"How do you like your fish prepared?" She saw that the biggest fish were probably two feet long. "Fried or baked?"

Billy squeezed his eyes and gathered his brows together. "I like them best fried, but these are probably too big for any fry pan we have."

Rachel smiled and ruffled the brown hair so much like his father's. "Then I guess we'll just have to cut them in half."

Billy gave her a radiant smile. "Good, then I'd like them fried."

"You help your father with the wagon, and I'll get the fish ready for cooking. I see you've gutted them. Good. That will save me time. I'll start cooking them a couple of hours before dinner Besides, I can keep an eye on Lucky this way."

"Lucky?" Billy's eyebrows wrinkled.

Rachel smiled and put her arm around

the boy's shoulders, careful to avoid the scales. "Yes, come see. Set the string of fish in the sink first, please."

They walked to the sink and Rachel helped him put the heavy string inside. Then she took him to the stove.

Lucky was still in pain, but there beside her, barely visible in her dark coat, was a tiny black puppy.

"Puppies!" Billy bent over and started to reach down.

Rachel put her hand on his arm. "Not yet, Billy. Let her finish having all of them, let her bond with them before we get our scent on them."

Lucky looked up at Billy and barked when he came near her puppy. When he stood back, she settled down. Plus she was again writhing in pain.

"Okay. Can I watch her?" He never took his eyes from the dog.

"Even though I'm pleased that she delivered the first pup on her own, she's tiny and I want to make sure she doesn't have any trouble with the rest of the puppies. If she looks like she's not delivering properly, I might have to help her."

He sat on the floor next to the box with

the dog and the puppy.

Lucky seemed to ignore him now and was licking her baby getting him or her free of all the after birth. Once the puppy's hair dried Rachel bet it would be dark brown not black as it looked wet. The tiny pup seemed to be the spitting image of its mother right down to the white socks on her back legs.

When the second puppy came, Lucky cleaned and cared for it as well. Then came a third and a fourth. Lucky was behind in the cleaning process, and the little pups were not able to get out of the birthing sacks themselves.

Rachel picked up the wet puppies and carefully removed the filmy sacs before putting the babies down for their mother to see and to care for. Her heart filled with love for each of the little animals, she didn't think she'd be able to give them away when they were older.

Lucky looked up at Rachel as if to say *thank you*, just before she started to whine and her body writhed around.

"That puppy isn't coming out like the others." Billy pointed at the pup only half way out and not moving. "Is she going to die like my mama did?" He looked up at Rachel with tears in his eyes.

Rachel put her arm around Billy, heedless of the scales on his shirt. "No, Billy. She'll be fine. The puppy is just a little stuck. We'll give it just another minute or so before I help her and pull the puppy. It's best if she delivers on her own."

Jason had been unloading the wagon and must have heard Billy's question because he came over and knelt next to his son.

"This is nothing like when your mama died. Rachel will help Lucky, and she'll be fine." He gazed up at Rachel, one eyebrow lifted. "Isn't that right, dear."

"Yes, it is. The time has come." Rachel gently grasped the little dog's rear end with her fingers and pulled it from its mother. She removed the sack and put it down with the other puppies next to Lucky.

The first puppy found Lucky's teats and was nursing. The rest were looking hard. One of them had no sense of direction at all, moving farther away from its mother.

Rachel turned the pup around and headed it in the right direction.

"Shall we find out what sex these little darlings are? I'm tired of calling the babies *it*. This can be a little difficult at this age, but

I'll give it a shot." She picked up the black nursing pup, looked underneath it and declared, "It's a boy."

Rachel identified the gender of each puppy. The litter had three males and two females. The three male puppies were black, dark brown and the last was the only golden baby. Of the female puppies one was black and the other, was the firstborn dark brown one. The black male pup and the dark brown female had white socks like their mama, but the others were solid colored.

"Would you like to name them, Billy?" Rachel put the little one with no sense of direction back at his mother's teat.

A big smile crossed his face. "Really? I can do that?"

Billy's excitement made Rachel believe that, like her, the child had never had a pet before.

"Sure. Remember just watch for now."

Billy frowned. "But you picked up every puppy, and their mom doesn't seem to mind any."

Rachel gathered her eyebrows together. "No, she didn't, did she? All right, but let them eat first. Then you can take care of them while I bathe mama."

She noticed that the one wayward black puppy was shoving her brothers to get at the nipple they had. She picked up the pup and set her back at the original teat. She sucked for a moment or two and then pushed at her siblings again.

"Jason, I don't think Lucky has enough milk for all these puppies. She has at least one dry teat. Watch." Again she moved the puppy, and the result was the same. "We'll have to feed some of them ourselves."

He watched and shook his head. "I don't know how to feed a puppy or any baby animal for that matter."

She cocked her head. "Of course, you do. You fed Billy. The process is the same except because these puppies are so little, we'll have to use an eye dropper instead of a bottle. I'll show you how. Do you have an eyedropper?"

Jason walked to the cupboard to the right of the sink. "Yes, but I use it for laudanum. I don't think it would be a good one for use with the puppies."

"No, we'll have to get a new one." Rachel turned toward Billy. "Would you like to go to the mercantile for me and buy two eyedroppers? Then when you get back, you and I will feed the two smallest puppies. Sound like a deal?"

Billy grinned, his eyes were bright with excitement. "Yes, ma'am. I'll be right back. I'll ride Jude. He lets me ride him bareback."

"Jason, will you give him the money for the eyedroppers, please?"

"He doesn't need it. We have store credit." He turned to Billy. "Just tell Fred to put them on our bill."

"Okay."

Billy raced out the door.

Once he was gone Rachel turned toward Jason. "I don't know if we'll be able to save the littlest pups or not. They need mother's milk for the first twenty-four hours if possible, but that's not happening this time. Do you have any milk? I should heat it before Billy returns."

Jason retrieved the milk from the icebox and got her a pan from one of the cupboards under the counter. "Here you go. I'll make sure the fire is stoked in the stove."

Rachel poured about a cup of milk into the pan. The amount was way more than both puppies could eat, but the higher amount would heat more evenly. She placed the pot on the stove and stirred the milk so the liquid wouldn't scald or burn.

By the time Billy returned with the eyedroppers, the milk was cooled and ready to use.

"Miss Davison said to give this to you." Billy handed Rachel an envelope.

"Thank you, Billy. Okay, here is one of the little black pups. She's a girl so you can think of a name while you feed her. Put her on your lap on her stomach. Take the eyedropper and put it to the side of her mouth and squeeze a little. When you see that she's taking it you can press more. Keep doing that until she turns away her head indicating she's full, probably after about twelve or thirteen times.

"When I learned how to do this it was with kittens. We had barn cats, and my dad didn't care about them, but I did. I loved every one of those cats. They were as close to a pet as I had, so when I saw the mother push one of the kittens away, I brought it inside. My mother is the one who showed me how to feed the kitten. Unfortunately for me when the baby was weaned off of the milk and eating solid food, Father made me take it back to the barn."

Billy did precisely as Rachel showed him. The little girl pup was very hungry. She was the one with no sense of direction, and she ate fifteen eyedroppers of milk.

"Now place the puppy on your shoulder and rub her back, kind of like burping a human baby. Puppies need to be burped, too, so all the air gets out of their tummy otherwise air is painful for them."

She watched Billy follow her directions, rubbing the puppy's back with his hand. The pup made a noise.

"She burped." Billy wore a huge smile on his face. "She actually burped."

"Now you can hold her on your lap and pet her for a little while, and then she needs to go back in with her littermates, so she keeps nice and warm. Then we do this all again in about two hours. Are you up for it?"

Billy nodded so fast Rachel was glad his head was attached to his neck.

"Yes, ma'am. I like feeding the babies."

"Good. I need some help during the day, but I will do it at night. I want you to get your sleep. Okay?"

Billy glanced up at his dad.

Rachel could see Jason had cocked an eyebrow in that, 'don't fool with me' stance of his.

"Yes, Rachel. I'll only feed them during the day."

"Good. After about a month the puppies won't need night feedings anymore, as long as we feed them about four times during the day with the last feeding about ten o'clock at night. Now, though, I need to give mama there a bath and a haircut."

When Rachel first lifted Lucky, she whined. Rachel knew she didn't want to be separated from her babies. She started to growl.

"Hush now. Your babies are fine. You're getting a bath, and you'll feel much better when I'm done. I promise."

Washing Lucky was quite the task, and it turned out she wasn't black at all. Once Rachel got all the massive mats of hair cut out she retook the scissors and cut the coat short all over. Turned out Lucky's fur was light brown with streaks of black except for the white socks on her back legs. She was very perky without all that nasty hair, but she didn't bark.

Rachel thought maybe Lucky had brought her together with Billy, too. They seemed to have bonded over the dog and the puppies. Rachel was grateful for that because she didn't know if she'd been able to reach Billy otherwise. Even though they had talked a bit when he ran away, he was still standoffish around her. *This could definitely be the help I was looking for.*

Once she was finished with the dog, she checked her pin watch and realized she was behind and needed to start cooking the fish right away. The smallest of the eighteen fish Billy caught was twelve inches and the largest, twice that. All of them had beautiful pink meat and would taste wonderful.

Jason and Billy went out to the barn. Billy still had to take care of Jude and Jason had to take care of the wagon and the horses.

She searched the kitchen until she found the lard and the cornmeal. Several cast iron skillets hung on the wall behind the stove. Rachel took down the three biggest ones.

After mixing two cups of cornmeal with one teaspoon of salt, she put the fish through an egg wash, then the cornmeal and then fried them until the flesh was firm when she picked up the fish with a spatula. As the fish were done, she put them on a large cookie sheet in the oven to keep warm and cook a little more if needed.

In between cooking the fish, she checked for vegetables and found potatoes in one cupboard. She peeled two potatoes for each man and one each for herself and Billy. When all the fish were done, she scraped out the fish drippings and added fresh lard to the skillets to fry the potatoes. When the grease was melted, she added the sliced potatoes to the skillets and let them brown.

In the same cupboard with the potatoes were jars of green beans and cans of peas and of carrots. She selected the carrots and opened four cans into a large saucepan on the counter since it would only take a few minutes for the vegetables to heat.

While the potatoes were frying, Rachel remembered the note from Lucy in her pocket. She pulled it out and read it.

Dear Rachel,

I'm glad you're back and hope you had a wonderful trip. I kept watch on Glynnis and Nicole as you asked. Nicole spent money as usual, but I found out she's from a rich family and had all her savings with her when she ran from an arranged marriage.

Glynnis, on the other hand, met with the sailor the same night you left. I heard her say she'd see him again on Wednesday which is tonight. Maybe we can catch them red-handed.

I think we need to have the sheriff there, but I'd hate to have him come and the sailor not show up. I went to his office, but a notice on the door said he was in Tacoma for the next two days.

What do you want me to do? I'll meet you on the outskirts of town tonight at ten. See you then.

Lucy

What a dilemma. She had puppies to care for, men to feed and a husband to answer to. She'd have to talk to Jason…but what if he told her she couldn't go? She'd come too far to be denied the satisfaction of finally being right about a case. They would catch Glynnis and the sailor and then go to the sheriff.

But what if they wouldn't come with her and Lucy? The situation wasn't such that she and Lucy could overpower Glynnis and the sailor and make them go anywhere. Maybe she needed Jason, after all, …and the sheriff, too.

CHAPTER 11

After supper and feeding the pups again, Rachel approached Jason.

"May I have a word with you, please?"

"Certainly." He put down the Washington Standard newspaper he'd picked up in Olympia and met her gaze.

"Outside, please."

Jason cocked an eyebrow but followed her.

Flashing a smile, she sat on the porch swing and patted the seat next to her.

He sat and put his arm around her shoulders.

"You know that I suspect Glynnis of stealing the jewelry from the brides."

"Yes, I know of your suspicions."

"Well, she's meeting the sailor tonight. I want you to come with me and help us apprehend them."

He took his arm from her shoulders and put his hands together. He leaned forward resting his elbows on his knees and letting his clasped hands hang between them. "You know how I feel about you pursuing this and yet you continue."

"I have to see it finished." *If this is my last outing as a detective, I want it to be on a high note. I love the puzzle that a mystery is and solving it is exhilarating, but I want my marriage to work, too. I have to admit I feel pain when I realize that Jason thought this was a silly game. Now he sees it as a danger and either way he wants me to quit. For him, I'll try.*

He sat up and pinched his nose between his eyes.

"I also think we should inform the sheriff. Will you come with me now?"

Jason crossed his arms over his chest. His eyebrows furrowed and a frown marring his firm, full lips. "We'll tell the sheriff, and then you will be done with this. No more playing detective."

"If we solve this mystery, then I will try to make it my last."

"Try? There is no try. You *will* make this your last, I demand it."

She stood and looked down at him.

"I thought you told Adam you didn't

want to be a tyrant. What has changed? And you know how I feel about you demanding anything of me. I don't like it and don't respond well."

Jason ran his hand behind his neck.

"Damn it, can't you see the danger you're putting yourself in? Not to mention poor Lucy."

She lifted her chin. "We're quite safe. I always carry my gun on these excursions."

Jason's eyes practically bugged out of their sockets. "Gun?! You have a gun!"

If Jason doesn't calm down, he'll have apoplexy.

Rachel put her hand on his arm.

"Calm yourself. I know how to use it. I took lessons in New Bedford before we left."

"Why would you take lessons on how to use a gun, a pistol I'm assuming or perhaps a derringer."

She stiffened her back. "The weapon is a .22 caliber pistol with six shots, and I'm quite good with it."

"I bet you are…when you're shooting at a target. Aiming at a man and shooting him is very different."

"I know that, and I'm not looking to

shoot someone. Hopefully, just seeing the weapon will be enough to scare the perpetrator into complying."

Jason looked skyward.

She saw his lips move but heard no sound. She watched him squeeze and release his fists several times.

"Why are you mumbling? I can't hear you."

"I'm counting backward from ninety-nine hoping I'll calm down before I reach one and strangle you."

Before she realized it, she took a step back and then corrected the mistake. "Why do you want to strangle me? I haven't done anything wrong. I refuse to let you intimidate me."

"I'm not trying to intimidate you. Believe me, you'd know if I was. I'm trying to get you to see reason. You shouldn't be chasing thieves in the middle of the night. That is the sheriff's job."

"I don't have enough to go on, and you know the sheriff will probably just sweep it under the rug like the authorities have before."

"Brand is a good man."

"He may be a good man, but he's still a

man."

"I don't know what you mean."

Rachel paced in front of Jason. *He may be a good man, but I wonder about his sheriffing abilities.* "Yes, you do. I know you've already gone to him with the evidence I have and he's done nothing. I need to catch them red-handed before he believes a woman, me, knows anything about catching a criminal."

"Well, what credentials do you have? Have you *ever* been right about the people you've chased before? I talked to Lucy. She's worried about you, too, but won't admit it."

"Why would Lucy be afraid? She's seen these miscreants in action with her own two eyes. What do you mean won't admit it?"

"Lucy didn't actually say she's afraid for you. Just that she doesn't want you to take things into your own hands…just like you plan on tonight. She loves you and has mentioned your previous escapades. Get Brand, Sheriff Kearney. Take him with you."

"I would if he was in his office, but he's off to Olympia for two days."

Jason let out a long breath and ran his

hand through his hair.

"Can't this wait?"

She stopped in front of him. "No. This cannot wait. What if this is the last time we get the chance to reclaim the jewelry? What if he hasn't sold them yet but is waiting for all of the jewels to sell as a package? Maybe he can get more money that way instead of a single piece at a time."

"Assuming you're right, I'll go…by myself…and apprehend them. I'll put the sailor and Glynnis in the jail and the sheriff can take care of the rest when he arrives back in town."

She shook her head. "You won't know if it's the same man she's been workin' with. I have to go with you. Besides, this is my mystery, my case, I'm the one who may have solved it, and I want to be there for the finish."

Jason threw his hand up in the air and walked to the other side of the porch. "You're an obstinate woman."

"And you're a stubborn man, but you lo…er…like me just the way I am, or you wouldn't have married me." *What was I thinking? I almost said love and that would be a big mistake. He doesn't think he'll ever love me, but I trust he already does. I have to believe that or I couldn't have married him...even as much as I love him.*

"What's on your mind, Rach? You're suddenly very quiet."

"I just thought that I've made my case and now you have to decide if you let me come with you or whether I go by myself after you've left."

Jason shook his head. "You'd do that, too, wouldn't you?"

"Yes, I would. It's that important to me."

He sighed. "Well, I'd rather have you where I can keep an eye on you than out there on your own where you can get in who knows what kind of trouble."

Relieved and grateful, she threw her arms around his neck. "Thank you." She pressed a chaste kiss on his lips.

He wrapped his arms around her and, when she would have pulled back from the kiss, he pressed his tongue against her lips and deepened it instead.

She melted into his arms, as she always did. Loving the feel of him, the taste of him. When he finally pulled away, she stayed with her eyes closed until she heard him chuckle.

"What?" She opened her eyes and looked at him smiling down at her. "What do you find so amusing?"

"When we kiss you often keep your eyes closed, as though you're committing the kiss to memory."

"That's exactly what I'm doing. Just in case you quit wanting to kiss me, I'll have these wonderful memories to carry me through."

His smile faded. "Why would I ever want to stop kissing you?"

I think I misspoke again. "I…I don't know. What if you find someone you can love? Won't you want to marry that person?"

His face clouded over. "That will never happen. Ever."

"You don't know that. Just because you can't love me doesn't mean another woman won't come along in the future and set your heart aflame."

"You're being ridiculous."

He let her go and turned to go back in the house.

Panic seized her. *Did I ruin my chance to succeed as a detective because I mentioned love?* "Where are you going? I thought we were going to town."

"We are. I'm getting my gun. I want to be prepared."

Rachel put her hand on her skirt over her pocket and felt her pistol, the weight of it comforting her. She, too, was prepared for whatever the night might bring.

*****

Jason couldn't believe he was actually accompanying his wife on her fool's errand to catch some thieves. Didn't Rachel realize she could be hurt? Or that she could injure someone she didn't intend? What in the hell was she doing with a gun? A husband's job is to protect his wife. Didn't she know that?

Now that he thought about it, she probably didn't know he would protect her and take care of her. After all, they'd only been married a short while, and she'd been taking care of herself before this. Well, she would just have to learn to let him handle everything, that's all there was to it. But for now, he'd let her come with him.

They walked down the road to town.

Lucy met them on the outskirts.

"Glynnis hasn't left yet. I was sure she would have gone to the rendezvous by now." She bit her lower lip. "Do you think I got the date and time wrong or maybe they saw me and wanted to throw me off their trail?"

Rachel hugged Lucy. She was always happy to see her best friend. "I don't know. Let's wait a little while."

Lucy wrapped her shawl a little tighter around her. The month was May, but the nighttime temperatures were still chilly. "Okay. How was Olympia? Did you have fun?"

Rachel glanced at Jason and saw a smile spread across his face. "Yes. We had a wonderful time. Jason bought me a sewing machine. I can't wait to show it to you. It's a beautiful piece of equipment. I'll be able to sew so much faster. You can use it, too, if you want."

"Oh, I'd love to," replied Lucy.

They waited and waited. Glynnis never left the dormitory.

Jason cocked his head to the side. "Ladies, I believe this is what they call a bust. Let's go home."

Rachel's shoulders sagged. "Unfortunately, he's right. Nothing is happening tonight. If you see or hear anything else, or someone realizes their jewelry missing, send me a note."

Lucy nodded and pulled her blue paisley shawl over her shoulders instead of around them, and covering her neck against the slight chill of the breeze off of Puget Sound.

She hugged Rachel. "Goodnight. I'll see you the next time you come to town. I'm gonna miss seeing you every day."

"I'm not far away. Just up the wagon road to the house. It's about a fifteen-minute walk going up but half that coming down. Jason can do it in five minutes, or so I've been told." Rachel looked up at her husband. "And Billy can do the round trip in about twenty minutes. Apparently, children have a lot more energy than we do. I think he runs both directions."

Jason nodded. "It's true. When I'm motivated, that is, not all the time." He took Lucy's hand and kissed the top. "Good night, Miss Davison."

Lucy giggled. "How very gallant, Mr. Talbot. Good-night."

She walked away toward the dormitory. Rachel and Jason watched until she'd gone inside and then turned toward home.

Jason took Rachel's hand in his. "I'm

sorry they didn't show up as you'd hoped."

"So am I, more so for Lucy than for me. They duped her, which means they know we're on to them. We'll have to be more watchful. I think they might move their purloined stash of jewels sooner than they planned."

An owl hooted in the distance, and the pull on her legs as she walked up the hill was uncomfortable. " Hopefully that forced activity will make them sloppy and we'll catch them. Where would they take them?"

Jason shrugged and shook his head. "No place around here. They'd have to go to Olympia. You said the man is a sailor. One of Clancy's?"

"I think so."

"So he could take them to San Francisco when the *Bonnie Blue* makes her regular run. If that's the case, the ship will be leaving the day after tomorrow on the morning tide and won't be back for a couple of months. They'll have to make their move before then, more than likely tomorrow night. They wouldn't risk being seen during the day."

Jason ambled up the hill to his home.

No, their home…and she was thankful

he did. The distance wasn't that great, but the trail was fairly steep.

By the time they reached the house, she was breathing heavily and feared the constant bump of the pistol against her thigh would leave a bruise.

"You'll get used to the walk, and it won't affect you so much. Come sit on the porch swing before we go inside."

She nodded and lifted her skirt to mount the stairs with Jason following.

They sat on the swing while she caught her breath.

"I hadn't realized how steep the road is, having only traveled it in the wagon or the buggy. You must think me terribly weak."

Jason put his arm around her shoulders. "No, not weak. The first time walking up the mountain is the worst. Every time after this will get better and easier."

Heart still beating fast, she leaned into him. "I'm glad to know that. I'd hate to think I'd feel like this all the time."

"If you want you can always take the buggy. Most of the time you'll be going for supplies anyway and will need it to carry them home."

"I need to get used to walking…just like

everyone else. I'll just walk to town every day until the trip doesn't wear me out anymore."

He squeezed her close. "You're doing fine. Let's go inside. I have some other ways I'd like to see you lose your breath."

Rachel gazed up at him. The light was too dim to actually see his eyes, but she was sure the orbs were twinkling with mischief.

"You truly are insatiable."

"Only for you."

She leaned back, cupped his jaw with her hands and brought down his head to hers, her greedy lips locking with his. His tongue pressed against her and she opened for him, accepting his tongue into her mouth as surely as she would his member into her body later.

Rachel pulled away and gazed upward.

"Take me to bed now."

"Yes, ma'am. My pleasure."

*****

Thursday, May 11, 1865

Someone pounded on the bedroom door.

"Jason. Jason. Get up. There's been a murder."

Rachel bolted upright at the word murder.

Jason grabbed his pants and shoved both legs into them, buttoning them up as he hurried to the door.

Adam stood on the other side, fist raised, prepared to hit the door again.

Jason ran a hand through his hair. "What are you talking about? Murder? Who?"

"One of the brides. She was found this morning badly beaten but wearing a shawl someone recognized as belonging to Lucy Davison."

"No!" shouted Rachel from the bed. Her eyes widened, and her throat got tight. "Not Lucy. That's impossible. We saw her last night wearing her shawl, blue—"

"With a paisley design," said Adam, finishing her sentence.

"Yes. Please go downstairs and wait for us, while we dress," said Rachel, with the sheet locked under her arms.

Adam nodded. "Of course. I'm sorry. I know she was your friend."

"She *is* my friend." Her stomach clenched. "That is not her. I will see the body for myself, but I tell you now, that person is not Lucy." *It simply can't be. I refuse to believe that Lucy is the corpse on the table at...where?* "Where is the body being examined?"

"Right now it's in Dolly's saloon."

"Will you see that the woman is transferred to the doctor's—"

Adam was as disheveled as she and Jason. His hair stuck up all over and he resembled a rooster "We don't have a doctor. That's why the body's in the saloon."

"Never mind," said Jason. "Give us a few minutes, and we'll be down." He shut the door.

Fighting back tears, Rachel bounded out of bed and began dressing.

"It's not Lucy." *Please, God, don't let it be Lucy.*

CHAPTER 12

As they left the house, Jason headed toward the barn, presumably to get the buggy.

Rachel couldn't wait. She picked up her skirts and began to run down the trail toward town. Didn't he understand she had to make sure the dead woman wasn't Lucy? Hitching up the buggy would take too long. She had to know now.

"Rachel," he called after her. "Wait."

She didn't stop or even slow down. She needed to know and only she would. Only she could prove that the body was not Lucy's.

Jason got the buggy and caught her about halfway to town.

He stopped the horses in front of her, slowing her. Then he jumped out and grabbed her arm as she tried to pass.

She pulled against his grip, but he didn't relax.

"Let me go. I have to see. That corpse cannot be Lucy, it just can't be. We saw her. Made sure she was in the dormitory. Safe."

She couldn't hold back the tears any longer and sagged against Jason, his flannel shirt crushed in her hands as she cried into his chest.

Jason wrapped his arms around her and held her against him. "Shh. Everything will be all right," he mumbled into her hair as he put his cheek against her head.

Rachel didn't know how long she stayed like that. Crying. Wetting his shirt with her tears. He tried to ease her fears and didn't let her go but held her as long as she needed him to.

Finally, she stepped back and used the handkerchief from her left skirt pocket, to dry her tears and blow her nose.

"I'm all right now. Let's get this over with so we can begin searching for Lucy."

"You truly believe this body is not Lucy? How will you identify her? Adam said she is unidentifiable except for her shawl."

"If her body is intact and the killer only

destroyed her face, I'll know. Lucy has a birthmark on her back. No one else knows." She tugged on his hand. "Let's go, and you'll see, the poor woman on the table in Dolly's saloon won't have that birthmark."

They climbed into the buggy for the two minute ride down the mountain to Dolly's Saloon. Hurrying inside, Rachel saw Karen Martell standing by the body, but a blanket covered the mound so onlookers couldn't see anything.

"I want to see her, now, please." Rachel's throat was so tight she didn't think she'd be able to say the words.

"Are you sure? She was pretty badly beaten."

"Yes, only I want to see her back."

Karen cocked her head and frowned at Rachel's request. She unbuttoned the dress on the body, removed the chemise and corset, turned her over and revealed the woman's *unblemished* back.

Rachel let out the breath she'd been holding, and her body sagged. The victim wasn't Lucy. She turned to Jason and pressed a hand to his arm. "It's not her. I told you the woman wouldn't be Lucy." Returning her attention to Karen, she asked,

"Who else is missing."

"Glynnis. We assumed she ran off with the sailor she'd been meeting."

"You knew about that?"

Karen nodded and smiled. "Her meetings with the sailor was the world's worst kept secret. Everyone knew…at least every bride I spoke with knew."

Rachel looked from Karen to Jason. "I'd bet my last dollar this is Glynnis and Lucy has been kidnapped. We have to find her before that man decides to do away with her as well."

"What makes you think he hasn't already?" asked Jason.

Rachel opened her arms wide and looked around, wide-eyed. "There's no body. I think he's holding her as insurance against being caught."

Jason paced the floor in front of the body which Karen had covered again. "He can't sail with Clancy. He's got to know he's a person of interest in Glynnis's death—"

Rachel stopped his progress with a hand to his arm. "And finding him would be too easy. I think he's headed to Olympia. You said that was the closest place to get rid of the jewelry."

"If you're right, he has a few hours head start on us." He held Rachel by the arms. "I want you to stay here with the brides. You can interview them and see if they know anything else about Glynnis—"

Even before all the words were out of his mouth, she began shaking her head. "No. I'm going with you. Lucy will need me, and I can ride a horse as well as any man here. I can shoot him, too, if I have to. Nothing will keep me from helping Lucy. If you don't let me come with you, I'll follow on my own. You know I will."

He closed his eyes and let out a breath. "You'll be the death of me."

Rachel put her hands on her hips. "I won't be left behind. Not now. Not ever, so you might as well get used to it."

"Fine. Let's get the horses and a warrant from Alfred Pope. As the mayor he can issue one for Harvey Long's arrest."

An hour later she and Jason galloped down the road toward Seattle. Rachel wished she had pants to ride in. First, she'd be warmer and second, she disliked showing her legs, but there was no choice. The weather had been mild for early May, and she was glad of it because the wind whooshing past her ear was more than cold enough. None of that mattered, though. Right now getting to Lucy was paramount. She kicked the sides of Star, the roan gelding she rode. Jason assured her the horse was the gentlest he had. But the animal hadn't wanted to take the bit, and Rachel had to force the metal past his teeth.

When she mounted, the horse started to buck. She held the reins tight and squeezed with her legs to keep from being unseated. Finally, Star settled down and was ready to take her wherever she needed to go.

"You're weight is too slight. The gelding doesn't act like that with any of the men."

"I'm fine. Star didn't unseat me, and now he knows who's the boss."

When they got into town, dozens of men were gathered in the saloon, waiting to ride after the perpetrator. Rachel knew each man was anxious to make a good impression on one of the brides.

The sheriff was still out of town, supposed to be in Tacoma, so Jason took charge. He raised his arms and waved them down while shouting over the din of crowd noise. "Men. Quiet down. Quiet down."

Slowly, the racket subsided, and he no longer had to shout.

"We're headed out after a dangerous man. He's already murdered one woman and may not hesitate to kill again. If you come upon him with Miss Davison, don't approach. Wait for Rachel and me. Rachel believes she may get him to let Lucy go without bloodshed."

"What if we get there and he's hurtin' Miss Lucy?" asked someone from the back.

"Then he'll answer to me," said Drew Talbot stepping forward from the crowd.

Rachel raised her eyebrows at Jason.

He shook his head and shrugged.

Well, this is an exciting turn of events. I hope Drew doesn't have reason to have the sailor answer to him. Please God, let Lucy be all right. Keep her safe.

Jason chose ten men to accompany him, Rachel, Drew and Gabe. Michael and Adam would stay in town and keep watch over Billy. If something happened to him or Rachel or, God forgive, both of them, Billy would still have a family to care for him.

The posse of fourteen riders took off at a gallop toward Olympia, sixty miles south of Seattle. Sneaking up on the sailor and Lucy unawares was impossible. The noise the riders made sounded like thunder coming down the road through the forest.

Jason had them alternating between galloping and trotting to keep the horses from becoming winded. At those gaits, the sixty miles took them just over five hours of hard riding. Enough of a lag behind the sailor and Lucy that they never caught up to them.

Rachel stood in the stirrups, giving her bum a rest. Apparently, her body had forgotten how to ride a horse because it was protesting now.

She seated herself again and pulled up next to Jason. "What do we do?"

They'd reached the edge of town and slowed the horses to a walk.

Rachel gazed all around, looking for Lucy.

Jason tipped his head to the right. "We go to the sheriff's office and report the information that we have. He'll know the easiest place to fence the stolen jewelry."

The posse followed Jason to the lawman's office. Jason came around to help Rachel down from the saddle.

But she was on the ground by the time

he got there.

She read the sign to the right of the door. "Sheriff Steven Westbrook."

Above the door was a sign that read "Sheriff's Office and Jail."

Jason rapped on the door and opened it without waiting for an answer. He and Rachel entered, leaving the rest of the posse outside.

The office was rather small and contained a desk and chair, a second chair in front of the desk and a potbellied stove with a coffee-pot on top. The wall to the right of the desk was full of wanted posters.

A man she assumed was the sheriff stood with his back to them, nailing up a new poster.

"Sheriff Westbrook?" Jason stood beside Rachel his arm around her waist.

"I'm Steven Westbrook," the man answered without turning around but finished his job. "What can I do for you?"

Finally, he lowered the hammer, and walked behind the desk, setting the tool on the corner.

Rachel, anxious to find Lucy, didn't wait for the sheriff to exchange pleasantries. "We need to find my friend."

The man didn't wear a hat inside though a black Stetson hung from a peg next to the right side of the door, easy to reach as he left the office. Pale blond hair spilled over his collar like he'd missed a haircut or two but he wore a goatee that was extremely neat and precisely cut. Hard, whiskey brown eyes peered at them from behind dark brown eyelashes and under brows raised in question.

The sleeves of his white shirt were rolled up to the elbows, and the brown leather vest could have been out of place with his denim pants, and yet it suited him. A revolver filled the holster on his hip and, in Rachel's opinion, he looked like he knew how to use it.

"I'm Jason Talbot." He pointed to her. "This is my wife, Rachel. We're from Seattle and chasing a man wanted in connection with the murder of one woman, kidnapping of another, and the theft of jewelry from many of the women that were brought in as brides."

The sheriff lifted his chin, pointing it at Jason. "I heard about that. Shipped in one hundred women to marry your lumberjacks and mill-workers. You did much better than

Asa Mercer did."

Jason crossed his arms. "That's correct. Can you help us recover the woman and the jewelry, hopefully before Harvey Long sells the jewelry or murders our friend, Lucy Davison?"

Sheriff Westbrook stroked his beard into a point. "I'll still need a written warrant to arrest him for murder."

Jason pulled the writ he'd gotten from Alfred Pope. "I've got one right here from our mayor, but you won't need it if you catch him in the act of selling the stolen goods would you?"

The sheriff raised his finger. "No, but he could claim they are his."

Rachel couldn't stand it any longer. "We can prove the items don't belong to him, but we need to find him to get my friend back. The stolen items are secondary. He's killed one woman. I don't want to give him the chance to kill a second."

Seemingly satisfied, Sheriff Westbrook nodded. "We need to see Sammy Chong. He's the biggest fence in the county, in more ways than one. The man probably weighs four hundred pounds. He also covers his ass." The sheriff looked down at Rachel.

"Forgive my crude language."

Rachel waved away the sheriffs words. "Nothing to forgive. I understand and probably would have said the same thing myself."

"Let me get my horse, and I'll take you there, but just the two of you." He pointed at Jason and Rachel. "The rest of your men can stay here or go across the street to the Dry Creek Saloon. Miss Joanie will welcome them with open arms."

"I'll tell them." Jason stepped out of the office and left the door open.

The sheriff turned his attention to Rachel. "So, Mrs. Talbot, is some of the jewelry yours? Is that why you're here with your husband?"

"Yes, but I'm here mainly for my friend, the kidnapped woman. I'm here to make sure we get her back safely. My grandmother's necklace is unimportant compared to Lucy's safety."

"You don't think your husband would do that, get her back, I mean?"

"I'm sure he will, but I need to be here for her. This experience has to be harrowing."

"Are you sure you don't have another

reason?"

She felt a little guilty for fibbing, but the gun hidden securely in her pocket made her feel safe. "What other reason could there be?"

"I don't know, but that pistol in your pocket doesn't bode well for either the perpetrator...or you if you pull it out of there." He jutted his chin toward her skirt.

"I assure you, Sheriff, I know how to handle this weapon." She patted her thigh. "And I will not let the man get away just because I'm a woman and shouldn't know those kinds of things."

"In my experience, a woman does not carry a weapon or chase after kidnappers. What else don't I know?"

Rachel lifted her chin. "You know everything except how this man killed the woman in Seattle. He beat her to death, smashing her face so much that she was quite unrecognizable. I don't want him to do that to my friend, and I will stop him if I can."

"I see," said the sheriff.

Jason returned from sending the men to the saloon. Drew followed him in.Dr

Jason shook his head. "I'm not sure that

was a good idea. They're all going to be too drunk to be of much use."

The sheriff nodded toward Drew but spoke to Jason.

"Mr. Talbot, I thought I made myself clear only you and your wife are to accompany me."

Shaking his head, Jason put up his hand. "Easy, Sheriff. Drew has a special interest in this situation. I'd like him to come along."

"Sheriff." Drew extended his hand.

Sheriff Westbrook shook it.

"I have a special interest in this...situation," said Drew.

Rachel was pleased that Drew was coming along. If she couldn't reach Lucy, maybe Drew could.

The sheriff didn't look pleased but sighed. "All right. You can come but no one else. I don't want to look like a mob descending on Sammy. He'll suddenly speak no English, as sure as the sun's in the sky."

"He's the last of our group. We're following you, Sheriff," said Jason.

"Get your horses and meet me out back." He pointed out the back door. "That way is the closest and the least conspicuous."

Jason, Rachel and Drew hurried out the front door and mounted their horses, meeting the sheriff behind the jail.

The group rode south to the edge of Olympia proper and entered the Chinese settlement. In what appeared to be the middle of homes and businesses alike was a two-story building. The sign on it proclaimed *Sammy Chong's Imports*.

The Chinese people stopped what they were doing and watched the riders. None of them smiled or looked welcoming in any way. They didn't want Rachel and her party here in their town.

The sheriff reined in, dismounted and wrapped the reins around the hitching rail in front of the whitewashed structure.

Rachel saw the porch of the building was full of statues of a fat man, smiling and sitting cross-legged. The pieces were porcelain, bronze. She thought the bronze would discolor in the damp weather, but that didn't appear to be the case.

The Talbots followed suit and dismounted, too.

"Follow me and let me do the talking. You understand? Not a word." He looked directly at Rachel and pointed. "Especially you. Women have no value in Chinese culture except as chattel. I can tell by your eyes that you don't like that fact, but now is not the time for that discussion. Got it?"

"Yes, sir." Rachel didn't like this Sammy Chong already and couldn't even tell him so. She fumed inside, but she wouldn't risk Lucy's life just to express her opinion to someone who wouldn't listen anyway.

They walked up half a dozen steps, crossed the crowded porch and entered through a door into another world. The room was so dark Rachel could barely see anything. Her eyes had trouble adjusting from the bright sunshine outside to the dark inside.

The sheriff walked through the room as though he had no trouble seeing. Either that or he had everything memorized from previous visits. She was afraid she'd lose him in the clutter of vases, rugs, bronze figurines and other treasures covering just about every surface.

They entered the back room where a Chinese man, looking to weigh about four hundred pounds, sat in a large rattan chair. How the fragile-looking wood held him, she had no idea.

"Ah, Sheriff Westbrook, what bring you to Sammy Chong? Surely you last visit gave you all *carpets* you need for you new home."

Sheriff Westbrook ignored the bribe innuendo. "These folks are looking for a sailor selling some jewelry. The jewelry is stolen." The sheriff cocked an eyebrow, "And I know you don't want to get involved with anyone selling you stolen items."

Rachel didn't think the enormous man cared in the least one way or another whether it was stolen jewelry. He just didn't want to get caught with it.

"Young man come here." He pointed at the floor where the sheriff stood. "He try sell me mother's jewelry. Ugly brooches and necklaces mostly. Nice stones. Ugly setting. Not beautiful like jade. I tell him come back at midnight."

"Midnight? For a legitimate jewelry sale? Come on Sammy. Even I don't believe that. Give me his name and where he's staying."

The Chinaman shrugged, his girth jiggling with the movement.

He narrowed his eyes. "Maybe my boys

follow sailor. What it worth to you?"

The sheriff frowned and took a step forward. "Letting you stay in business. Where's he at Sammy?"

At the sheriff's movement, Sammy was quick to answer, putting up his hands in front of him. "Okay. Okay. He say he store package at hotel for he come back."

"Package? What package?"

"Boys say black hair woman in room," Sammy shook his head, setting his three chins to jiggling. "But her not want be there. They say she kick sailor then he hit her in the face. Put her in place. She fell to floor and did what he say."

Beaten! Rachel couldn't stand it and didn't give a damn if Sammy liked it or not.

"Where? What hotel? Please answer me."

Sammy Chong stared at her.

"You dare speak in my presence? We done." He mimed washing his hands as he spoke to Sheriff Westbrook. "You not control your females, how I trust you control anything else?"

Jason jabbed her in the side and frowned.

"Wait. Sammy. The female doesn't

know what she's done. She is stupid, like all females"

The sheriff glared at Rachel.

She looked from the sheriff to Jason, to Sammy and realized she might have jeopardized their chance for the information. She'd give the man a piece of her mind at another time.

"One hundred dollars for name of hotel," said Chong with finality.

Sheriff Westbrook looked back at Jason and Drew.

"That's fair don't you think men?" the sheriff asked them with his eyebrow cocked and his lips in a straight line.

"Of course." Jason pulled the money out of his pocket and handed the sheriff the bills.

The sheriff stepped forward and gave the cash to the Chinaman.

"Any of the jewelry that you may have already bought, we'd like to buy back," said Jason.

Chong shook his head. "Not buy any, was for tonight. Now not possible. Westbrook, you keep our arrangement. Stay on you side of town. You bad for business."

"We can't have that." The sheriff

nodded. "Except for circumstances such as these, I will abide by our agreement."

"Good. You go *Riverside Inn,* find what you seek. Leave."

Sheriff Westbrook bowed his head, and the rest of them followed his example.

As they left, Rachel heard laughter coming from the fat man behind them and wondered if he gave them the truth about where to find Lucy.

She didn't trust the laughing fat man who looked a lot like the statues on his porch.

CHAPTER 13

They followed the sheriff to the Riverside Inn. Rachel would have called it the Rundown Inn because it was decrepit. The building needed a fresh coat of paint, shutters, hanging by one nail, needed to be nailed to the wall again. The windows in the front doors were cracked, and the sign above the porch needed to be re-hung before it landed on someone's head. None of the rooms had balconies to look over the river

Once inside the sheriff went to the registration desk and spoke to the woman there.

"Hello, Della." He pointed toward the Talbots. "This is Mr. and Mrs. Jason Talbot and Drew Talbot. We want the room number for Harvey Long."

The red-haired woman in her forties looked at the book in front of her. "I don't have anyone by that name, Steven."

"I'll need to see the registration book."

"Certainly."

She turned around the book.

The sheriff ran a finger down it until he found what he was looking for.

"Here. Harve Smith. He's using a fake name. Room 229."

They all started toward the stairs.

"If you break it you bought it. Be careful with my door." Della called after them.

Outside the room, the sheriff pulled his weapon.

"Harvey Long. This is Sheriff Westbrook, open up."

A commotion sounded from inside the room.

The sheriff's shoulders dropped, and he shook his head.

"Why don't they ever just open the door?"

He stepped back then crashed in the door with his booted foot.

A stocky man with dark hair hesitated halfway out the window. Then he was all the way out and screaming as he fell two stories to the ground.

The sheriff hurried to the window and looked out. "He's not going anywhere. Looks like he broke his leg."

"Good. I wish it had been his neck," said Jason.

Rachel rushed to where Lucy lay tied up on the bed. Her face swelled, ugly black and blue bruises were forming, evidence of Long's violence against Lucy. Rachel first removed the gag and then tried to untie her.

"Here, let me." Drew took his knife from his boot and cut through the ropes. "There, that's better."

Rachel saw him extend his hand toward Lucy to help her up, but she turned her face away.

Drew looked at Rachel, his brows furrowed. Then he merely peered at Lucy before walking away.

"She'll come around. Give her some time," said Jason.

Rachel heard Jason try to console his brother, but wasn't sure Lucy's 'coming around' would be anytime soon. She was in complete disarray. Her dress was ripped and dirty, her hair—her glorious black hair— hung from the bun she usually wore and was a mess of tangles.

Rachel didn't know what had happened to Lucy, but it was clear that her friend was traumatized. Rachel's heart ached for her, she wanted to cry, but that wasn't what Lucy needed.

"Jason, you and Drew deal with the sailor outside. You can search the room for the jewelry, or beat the information out of him since that seems to be the only way he understands anything. Lucy will ride with me on the way home. If you would help us mount I'd appreciate it."

"Certainly. Whenever you both are ready," said Jason.

She gazed over at Lucy. "We'll go now. Needless to say, the ride home will be much slower than the one here."

Lucy had sat up when Rachel was next to her but hadn't moved from that position. She simply stared at the wall in front of her, though Rachel didn't think she actually saw anything, her gaze was hollow.

Rachel stood, took Lucy's hand and helped her to stand. "Lucy, let's go home now." Together they walked downstairs to the waiting horses, followed by Jason and Drew.

"Back to New Bedford?"

Lucy turned her head toward Rachel. Her voice raised as though in anticipation of something good about to happen.

Rachel put her arm around Lucy and wrinkled her brows, knowing the answer would not please Lucy. "No, dear. Back to Seattle."

She shook her head and shrugged off Rachel's hand. "No. I want to go home, Rachel. All the way home. Back to Massachusetts."

A sudden coldness hit Rachel at her core. "You don't mean that. You don't want to be under your father's thumb again. Nothing for you remains there. We are here, you and I. Seattle is where you belong. With me."

Lucy spoke. Her voice quiet, like she was afraid to be heard.

"I followed Glynnis just like I'd done before. She met with *him,* and they started shouting at each other. Then he hit her. She fought back as long as she could, but he knocked her against a wall and then to the ground." Lucy stopped and gulped air. "He smashed her face into the ground again and again. Her lovely face was no more only a mass of blood and broken bones. That's when I knew she was dead, and I was glad for her. I must have gasped or made some other noise because he looked up and saw me. I tried to run, but he caught me."

She stopped only to take a breath.

"He took my shawl and—"

"Stop dear." Rachel put her arm around Lucy's shoulders. "We know what happened. You don't need to relive that."

Rachel was afraid if Lucy relived the horror, it would affect her badly and she'd been through enough without having to relive it

Lucy seemed not to have heard Rachel. "I'm surprised he didn't kill me on the way here."

Her voice was flat as she spoke and the sound made chills run up Rachel's spine. Lucy was in trouble. This person was not the Lucy she knew. The woman in front of her was a hollow shell of her dear friend.

Rachel turned to Jason, who shook his head and frowned.

"Lucy." Rachel kept her voice soft. "I'm going to help you onto the saddle. Are you ready?"

She didn't answer, but went to the horse, grabbed the saddle horn and put her left boot into the stirrup.

Rachel pushed her at same time she pulled herself up.

Once she settled, she stared straight ahead again.

Rachel grabbed the back of the saddle and the horn put her foot in the stirrup.

Jason called her back. "May I speak to you for a moment?"

At Jason's words, she looked up at Lucy and nodded. "For just a minute."

"I'm having Drew go with you. He's worried about Lucy. I want you to go slow and let us catch up with you."

"All right. Is that all?"

"No. There's this."

He gathered her into his arms and gave her the tenderest kiss. She wrapped her arms around his shoulders and held him close.

His lips caressed hers, but he didn't press his advantage when she gasped. He pulled back and rubbed his thumb over her bottom lip.

"We have some talking to do when we get home."

"All right."

"I should go before Drew beats Long to a pulp, broken leg or not."

"Don't let him damage Long too much. He needs to tell us where the jewelry is and stand trial for Glynnis' murder."

"That's another reason Drew needs to go with you. The sheriff and I will find the jewelry, and I'll bring it home, along with Long. I'll catch you before you stop for the night. We aren't pushing the horses this time, and it's late enough now that we'll have to stop for the night."

She stood up on tiptoe and brushed her lips across his.

"I'll be waiting."

She walked to the horse where Lucy sat staring straight ahead.

Jason followed her and lifted her behind the saddle as though she was a child instead of a full grown woman. He was so strong, and at the same time gentle. He amazed her. Jason could easily use that power against her, but he never did.

"Thank you. Lifting me wasn't necessary, but," she grinned. "I do like to fly."

Rachel took the reins, turned the horse around, and headed the animal out of town wondering what would happen when the men caught up. Would Drew take matters into his own hands and could Jason keep the killer safe?

*****

By that evening when they stopped for the night at the livery in Tacoma, Jason and the other men had caught up.

Rachel knew the sailor had done more than just beat up Lucy. He'd destroyed everything she took for granted, paramount being her sense of safety. Lucy wouldn't leave Rachel's side, not even when she needed to relieve herself.

And Rachel knew this injury was her fault. If she hadn't wanted to catch Glynnis and Long in the act, Lucy wouldn't have been there.

When they were on their way back to the livery, Rachel stopped.

"Did Long do anything else to you?"

Finally, Lucy began to cry, and she shook her head.

"No. I was so afraid. He...he threatened to rape me, but never actually did the deed. He put his hands on me and ripped my dress…but that was all. He frightened me." She shuddered, her whole body shaking.

"Oh, honey." Rachel wrapped her arms around her friend. "Of course, you were. Your fear is normal. He kidnapped you, and he used terrible threats and violence to keep you docile. None of this is your fault."

Lucy blinked against flowing tears. "If I'd minded my own business—"

Rachel pulled back to arm's length. "That's poppycock. This predicament is my fault. You were following them for me, weren't you?"

Sniffling, Lucy nodded.

"You wouldn't have been there if I hadn't been so adamant about catching them in the act."

"You didn't ask me to follow them." She ducked her head. "Both you and Jason told me not to, but I did anyway."

Rachel struggled to keep her voice calm through the guilt she felt. "This is Long's fault, no one else's. He's the one who kidnapped you, beat you, and threatened you."

Lucy just nodded and stared ahead.

"What are you thinking, Luce?"

She slumped and stared at her hands. "I'll never be Drew's wife. That's all I wanted. I love him, you know."

"I know you do. But why can't you marry him?"

Lucy began to cry again

"I'm soiled at least everyone will think I am."

Rachel hugged her close, held her, and let her cry. She slowly rubbed Lucy's back and let her friend weep. When she stopped and pulled back from Rachel, they returned to the livery and resumed their places in the fresh hay that served as their bed.

"Rachel, don't leave me. Please."

"I'll be right here when you wake. Okay?"

"Okay."

Later that night, Rachel got up and left Lucy sleeping.

Jason was still up and waiting for Rachel to come to him. She didn't disappoint him.

"Hi." She lay down next to him.

"Hi, yourself. How is Lucy?"

"Not good." She stiffened. "That bastard didn't let just beating her up be enough, but he threatened to rape her, too. She's very fragile right now. I can't stay long."

"I know, but I'm glad you came. I need you, too." He rubbed his hand down her arm. "But I also realize that Lucy needs you more at this time."

She raised her hand and traced her husband's jaw. "Thank you. We have lots to talk about, but that is for later. For now, just hold me."

"Your wish is my command."

He pulled her close, and she turned into him, putting her hand on his chest and laying her head on his shoulder. She stayed like that for a while. Listening to his heartbeat, relishing in the closeness. Then she pulled away. "I have to get back. If Lucy wakes and I'm gone, she'll panic."

"At some point, she'll have to get used to you not sleeping with her. I'm not willing to give up my wife permanently. But I do understand her need of you now."

Rachel understood Jason's fear. "Don't worry. Lucy needs time to process everything and realize she's stronger than this horrible thing that has happened."

She sat up and then leaned down and kissed Jason. She wanted so much to tell him how much she loved him and that he meant the world to her, but she couldn't risk her heart like that. He had to say it to her first. Rachel had to know she was at least as necessary as Cassie. She didn't want him, or Billy, to forget Cassie, but Jason had to make room in his heart for Rachel and their eventual child.

"See you in the morning."

He stood with her and hugged her to

him. "I'll see you then. Be with your friend. She needs you now."

"Thank you for understanding."

"I do."

She clung to his hand until her steps forced their hands apart.

You've got to love me, Jason. I couldn't stand it otherwise. I know now I can't be in a loveless marriage. I thought I could but I can't. Why can't you believe that you love me?

CHAPTER 14

Two weeks later

Rachel didn't wish what happened to Lucy on anyone, but she was getting better. The time had come for Lucy to continue the healing process on her own. Rachel would still be there, for a while, but Lucy had decided there wasn't anything wrong with her. She wanted to pretend that the incident had never happened and that worried Rachel but only Lucy could determine what was best for her and fight to get back to normal. Rachel would be there for her as long as she could.

Jason walked to the dormitory where Rachel was staying with Lucy. She came out to meet him as she always did.

"Can we talk?"

She looked up at him. Dark circles marred his handsome face and a little of her resolve dissipated. "Of course. What would you like to talk about?"

"Us."

"Good. Me, too."

"I want you to come home. Lucy needs to learn how to get along without you."

"I agree, she does, but I don't want to leave her too soon, either."

"I understand that, but the longer you put it off, the harder the separation will be on her when you finally do come back home. To our home. Where you belong. Ah, hell." He ran a hand around the back of his neck. "I miss you. Seeing you for a few minutes alone every day is not enough. I want to hold you in my arms and have relations with you. I'm feeling like a bachelor again. I want us to be a family, and that means you live with me."

"I would like to come home, but I don't think I can. I don't want to live a life without love. Lucy can get along without me now. That's not the problem. She'll see me every day at least until I leave. I'm planning on moving to Olympia. Hopefully, I'll find work there. These are grown women, and they can survive without me to hold their hands. I need to find someone who can love me back."

Jason started to speak but didn't know

what to say. He felt like he'd been punched in the gut.

Rachel looked at him and then gazed down, her eyes filling with tears.

"Even with me expecting your baby, you can't find room for me in your heart, what about the baby, is there room for him?"

"Rachel, I…I don't know what to say." His eyes opened wide. "Wait, you're expecting?"

Closing her eyes, she shook her head. "I love you, would have been a good start. Goodbye, Jason."

She turned her back on him.

Suddenly, he understood. "You're pregnant? But we've only been married for about six weeks. How could that be? I mean Cassie—"

"I'm not her." She stiffened and whirled around. "When will you realize I'm not Cassie? I'm not like her, and I don't want to be her. It's time you made room for me." She pounded her chest. "Me, in your life and your heart. I'm not a substitute for her. I told Billy I don't want to take his mother's place, and that is still true, but I can't go on being your substitute for her, either. I need my place in your heart."

The fight Rachel had on her hands was different. How do you fight a ghost?

Jason put his hands on her shoulders and stood behind her. "Rachel, come home. You need to have a safe place to stay until the baby is born."

"I'll stay at the dormitory, like before we were married, until the baby comes and then I'll move to Olympia."

"Do you want the whole town to know our business?

She was so tempted. Tempted to see if she could get Jason to admit he loved her. He had to. She simply couldn't exist in their marriage otherwise. She took a deep breath and swiped at her cheeks with her palms.

"No, I don't want our dirty laundry out in the open. I'll return home but only until I can figure out something else to do. And you'll sleep on the floor. I won't sleep with you."

"I'm not sleeping on the floor."

"Fine, then I will. I won't be tempted to have relations with you. The next time we make love, it really will be making love, or we won't do it." *You'll have to tell me you love me before we make love. I don't want it just to be having relations.*

"Whatever you say."

*****

Jason walked toward home. He was given a reprieve and still had a chance to salvage his marriage. He still had a chance to keep his wife. All he had to do was convince her he loved her. But did he? He was afraid of losing her, and that concern had nothing to do with the baby. He didn't want to lose *her*. Rachel. She brought out the best in him, and Billy adored her now that they were raising the puppies together. They'd bonded, and Jason couldn't be more pleased. But what did he feel? Rachel was his wife, yes. He loved to make love to her, yes. He enjoyed talking to her, she was smart and didn't take any guff off of him, yes.

Did he miss her when she was gone? Yes. Does his heartache at the thought of losing her? Yes.

Do all those things add up to love? Did he love his wife?

Yes. He did.

*****

Rachel didn't know what to think. Ever since she returned home and told Jason she was expecting, he was very solicitous of her needs. He always made sure to be available to carry the milk pails into the house and pour them through the cheesecloth.

He came with her to town and carried everything she bought to the buggy before driving up the mountain to the house, even if the item was just a ribbon for her hair.

He even helped her carry the food to the table and do the dishes after meals.

Not that she didn't appreciate the help, but he was making her crazy, always being underfoot. He was almost as bad as the puppies who thought she and Billy were their mothers. Having five, six-week-old puppies underfoot was one thing, having a fully-grown husband acting the same way was another.

Since she'd been gone for a while, the little ones were like Lucy and afraid she would leave again. They stuck to her like glue until Billy came home. Thankfully, they were happy sleeping in Billy's room, and he was glad to have all five puppies and Lucky with him.

Jason was afraid he'd lose her, too, like he did Cassie and she didn't know how to make him believe that she was stronger than Cassie.

Long was behind bars. There was no

way he was escaping jail. Sheriff Kearney assured them Long would be guarded day and night, until the trial was over and his sentence passed, most likely he'd hang. She was safe, and so was Lucy. The jewelry was all recovered from the room at the inn in Olympia.

The time had come for her to talk to her husband. She found him in the living room with his brothers.

He sat in a chair reading last week's Washington Standard newspaper, as usual.

She went over to him. "Would you come to the kitchen, please."

He practically jumped out of the chair. "Of course. What do you need?"

She peered around at his brothers and whispered. "Just to talk in private."

Suddenly the room got quiet, and each of the men stared at her.

She looked skyward and then back at her brothers-in-law. "Will you all go back to what you were doing, please?"

Each of them reddened and looked to the side or up or anywhere except at her, but they immediately looked away and resumed their conversations.

Jason took her by the hand. "Come on.

The weather nice out and the moon is full, let's go for a walk."

"All right. Let me get my shawl."

"You won't need it. If you get cold, I'll warm you up." He waggled his eyebrows.

She shook her head and grinned. "You are a crazy man."

"Only about you."

Rachel stopped and cocked her head, sure she'd misheard him and yet hope fluttered in her chest. "What?"

"Come on, let's go."

They walked into the woods, by the light of the moon, to the place where the path to his and Billy's fishing spot branched off.

"Here's a good log to sit on." He put down his handkerchief on the tree trunk for her to sit.

She gathered her skirt and sat on the log.

"I wanted to talk about us. What do you want to talk about?"

"Us."

"You go first."

"I've done some thinking, and I realize that you're not Cassie, and though I loved her, she's gone."

Rachel looked down at her lap. She didn't want him to see the tears in her eyes.

Was he going to tell her he couldn't love again? Clenching her fists in her skirt, she tried to keep her feelings under control.

"I'm sorry you lost the woman you love."

"So am I. I mourned her for a long time. Too long. Rachel, look at me, please."

She shook her head. Her throat was so tight she didn't know if she could speak.

"Please."

"No. I can't bear for you to tell me you can never love me."

"Rachel." He lifted her chin with one finger until she met his gaze. "I'm not saying that, ever again. I love you, Rachel Talbot. I've been fighting the feeling. Unable to believe that I could feel that emotion." He sat next to her. "I didn't want to love you. I put Cassie between us because I couldn't face the fact that I love you, but that was also the reason I insisted on marrying you so quickly after we landed."

"You love me?" His proclamation echoed through her mind. She hadn't heard anything else he'd said. "You really love me? Are you not teasing me? Because I…I couldn't take that."

He clasped her hand. "It's no joke. I love

you more than I ever thought possible."

"How? When?" Hearing the one thing she hoped and prayed for, her eyes filled with tears. Her heart pounded so furiously in her chest she was sure he could hear the beat.

"I think I've loved you since our first rendezvous on the *Bonnie Blue*. I couldn't believe this beautiful woman wanted to meet me. But you were where you said you'd be, so I guess you did. I'm thankful every day that you were so forward as to come to me and want to watch the stars."

She leaned over and put her arms around his neck to pull him close. "I love you, too." Rachel found his lips in the dark of night and kissed him with all the love in her heart. Then she pulled back, keeping her arms where they were. "What made you decide this now?"

"Lucy. What happened to her...the kidnapping, the victim, could have been you. I'd have killed that sailor had I been Drew. He wanted to, so I sent him with you, away from the sailor. Then, all the time you've been away with Lucy, I was...jealous of her." He tightened his embrace. "I missed you, and I couldn't figure out why, until I admitted that I love you. Then all my confused feelings made sense."

"We've wasted a lot of time when we could have loved each other. Let's not waste any more." She smiled. "Take me home and make love to me."

"That would be my pleasure."

They walked back home, hand in hand and then made love, real love, for the first time.

Jason was so gentle with her, treated her almost reverently, which was nice but not what she wanted or needed. She needed to feel alive. Rachel wanted to put what happened to Lucy out of her mind but the fact she could have been in Lucy or Glynnis' place, was not lost on her.

Jason's clever fingers made circles around her breast, occasionally tweaking her nipple before moving on. "What are you thinking about?"

"How lucky I am. I'm sure I'm the luckiest person alive. I'm married to the love of my life, expecting your baby, in beautiful surroundings. I solved my first case, with your help, and we returned all the jewelry to the brides. Who could ask for more?"

"I'm the lucky one. You are smart,

loving, caring and beautiful to boot. You, poor thing, have to put up with me."

"I think I hear a tiny violin. Are you angling for a compliment?" She put her finger on her chin and pretended to think hard.

He chuckled and crushed her to him.

She laughed. "All right, I give. You are the most handsome man I know. You're gentle and caring but strong when you need to be. I know you will protect us." She placed a hand on her belly.

He covered her hand with his. "I will always protect you and love you. What do you think Billy will say when we tell him? We have to make sure he knows this baby is not taking his place in our hearts. He worries about that, about being replaced, and we need to reassure him."

"I know, and we'll do whatever we have to in order to make sure he understands and feels safe."

"Shall we get dressed and tell the family our news?"

"Isn't it too late? We'll tell them in the morning. I can't wait to see the looks on your brother's faces."

"This is Saturday night. They'll be up

and so will Billy. They'll be jealous and overjoyed. They are already envious of me finding you as I did."

"They'll find their wives. I'm sure of it."

"I know they will. Until then, let them be envious of me." He brushed a kiss along her temple. "I love you, darlin'."

"And I you."

They dressed and went down to the living room where some of the brothers and Billy were playing cards or reading.

Jason cleared his throat.

"We have something we'd like to share."

Rachel stood beside him, smiling, her gaze fixed on Billy.

"Rachel and I are expecting a child."

Cheers and congratulations filled the air. Jason's brothers came and clapped him on the back and kissed her on the cheek.

Billy stayed where he was, looking at the floor.

Rachel went to him.

"Billy. You're awful quiet. Aren't you happy about becoming a big brother?"

He shook his head. "I don't know nothin' about being a big brother."

"It's easy, but also a great responsibility.

This child will need all of us to help show it how to live. Just like the puppies needed us to help them grow. And as he or she gets bigger, they'll need someone to show them how to catch lightning bugs and the best place to fish. You'll have to show them what to do and how to do it. Teach them and help them grow up into a wonderful young man like you. Your Dad and I can't do it all. We need you, too."

"She's right son. This baby will need you most of all." Jason laid his hand on her shoulder.

Billy raised his eyebrows. "Me? What will it need me for?"

"Who else will take him fishing or teach him how to tie your favorite fly? Who will show him where your fort is in the forest or how to climb a tree?"

Rachel recognized that she and Jason were both parenting Billy. They were becoming a family. "That's right. And there will be other babies. I hope you have lots of brothers and sisters. When they get older, they'll help us make cookies at Christmas, just like you will help me this year. So many things that they will need you for, but mostly they will just need you to be there and help them up when they fall. Dust them off and let them go again. Can you do that?"

"Yes, ma'am." He tilted his head. "Rachel?"

"Yes."

"Can you be my mama, too?"

Her tears fell, well, leaked was the more correct term. She'd dreamed of this moment and hoped the time would come when Billy would want to call her Mama.

She had to swallow past the lump in her throat. "I would be greatly honored to be your mama."

She opened her arms wide. Billy stood and ran into them. Rachel held her son, resting her cheek on the top of his head, just as Jason rested his cheek on her head. They stood like that for a while, until one of the brothers cleared his throat.

Jason stepped back and then Rachel pulled away from Billy, but Jason stood between them with one arm around each.

They were a family. A loving family.

Who knew that her greatest wish would come true when she signed up to be a Seattle bride?

EPILOGUE

March 6, 1866
The Talbot home

Rachel stretched. Pain flashed across the small of her back, and she wondered if today would be the day her baby decided to make an appearance. She rubbed her belly. "Are you ready yet, little one? I'm certainly ready to meet you."

"As am I." Jason came behind her and wrapped his arms around her belly. "How are you today?"

"Tired and achy. I think today may be the one."

He stiffened. "Do you want me to get Karen? I'll send Adam to get her with the buggy. Are you sure you're feeling all right?"

"Be calm, my darling. I'm fine. I don't—"

Rachel started to say she didn't need Karen yet and then felt the warm gush of water between her legs.

"Oh! I guess you'd better get her. My water just broke." She picked up her skirt and stepped over to the table. Will you get some towels?"

Jason stood staring at her, mouth open and eyes wide.

"Jason." She clapped her hands. "Jason. Get me some towels."

His head snapped up. "Yes. Towels." He went to the new pantry and returned with several.

Rachel took them, spread them on the floor and used her foot to mop the floor and clean up the mess when he stopped her.

"I'll get this. You're going to bed."

"I don't need to go to bed yet, I…" A wave of pain rolled across her belly. "Oh, Jason!"

He scooped her into his arms and headed for the stairs.

"I'm not taking *no* for an answer."

Jason took the stairs two at a time, carrying her like he would a child—for which she was grateful. His strength always amazed her.

When they reached the bedroom, she wiggled in his arms.

"Let me down. I need to change into a nightgown."

He set her on her feet.

With quick steps, she went to the screen.

Using linens out of the commode, she wiped down her legs with a washcloth and the soapy water she'd made in the basin, then dried them with a hand towel. She threw the nightgown that hung on the screen top over her head and pulled it down over her distended belly. She felt like a beached whale like she'd seen in the Sound and knew she looked like one, too.

Rachel waddled over to the bed and climbed in to wait for her baby to make its appearance.

"The baby probably won't be here for quite a while, and I prefer if we talk or read or something other than sit and stare at one another."

He pulled the rocking chair close to the bed. "What would you like to talk about?"

She folded her arms over her belly. "Names. We still haven't chosen."

He looked at her, an eyebrow cocked. "I thought we'd decided on Edward and

Angelica. Have you changed your mind again?"

"I like Edward, but I'm not sure about Angelica. I don't want her to be called Angel."

"What would you like for her to be called?"

"Lucy."

"You said we shouldn't because they'd end up being called Big Lucy and Little Lucy."

"I know." She sighed and smoothed the sheet over her belly. "I know. You're right. We'll stick with Angelica."

He was quiet for a moment. "We could name her after my mother."

She tilted her head just a little. "I don't remember you ever mentioning her."

Jason shrugged. "I didn't. We had decided on Angelica so I didn't mention it."

"What was her name?"

"Abigail but Dad always called her Abbie."

She put her hand out for him to take.

Instead, he stood, came around the bed and crawled in beside her, enveloping her in his arms. "This position is a much nicer way to wait for our child."

"I agree." She turned as far as her tummy would let her and cupped his cheek. "I also think Abigail would be a wonderful name for our daughter."

"Have I told you lately that I love you?"

She chuckled. "Not lately." Rachel loved this game they played—who had said I love you last. Every time they played, she felt all warm inside.

He smiled. "Then I have been remiss. I mean to tell you every hour of every day."

"Once a day is sufficient."

He waggled his eyebrows. "Once a day is never enough with you."

She poked him in the chest. "We are talking about different things now. Oh!" Rachel held her stomach, bearing the pain and letting it pass.

"Are you all right?"

"Just a pain to say our child is on the way. Karen said we should time them to see how far apart they are. Do you have your pocket watch?"

"I do."

He palmed the watch and checked the time.

"It's two ten."

"When they get to about six minutes

apart, we should send for Karen. No need for her to be here before that."

"Very well. I'll keep the time."

A knock sounded on the door.

Rachel looked up. Billy stood there, white-faced.

"Billy, my little love. What's the matter? You look like you've seen a ghost."

"Uncle Adam said you're having the baby."

Rachel put out her arm and beckoned. "Come here."

Billy ran to the bed and Rachel wrapped her arm around his shoulders. She didn't care whether it was appropriate or not for him to be in the room.

"This is nice. I'm between my two men, waiting for our baby. I'm fine, Billy. Soon I'll start having labor pains, and when they come again, I want you to go downstairs with your uncles. All right?"

He nodded against her chest. "I just wanted to make sure you were okay."

"I'm terrific. I can't wait to meet our new baby and for you to meet him or her, too. Have you made up your mind what you want the child to be?"

"I'd like a brother, but having a little

sister would be nice, too. I guess I'll be happy either way. I can still show her all the same things I would to a boy. I'll teach her how to fish and catch frogs and lizards. How to catch fireflies and put them in a jar to make a lamp and—"

"Enough, please." Rachel leaned down and kissed the top of his head. "I think no matter what child we get, you will be a wonderful big brother. Now, I need for you to go downstairs with your uncles. Be sure and tell them that I'm fine. How'd you get past them anyway?"

"They started playing poker, and you know how they get."

She nodded. "That I do."

Billy stood. "I'll tell them." He ran toward the door, then stopped and turned around. "I'm glad you're okay…Mama."

Every time he called her Mama, Rachel's heart burst with happiness. The title was still new to both of them, so he tended to blush each time. That was okay…so did she.

After Billy was out of the room, Rachel grabbed Jason's arm.

"I'm having another. How long since the last one?"

"About six minutes. We should send for Karen. I'll send Adam with the buggy, but it will still take her a while to get here."

"Agreed."

He kissed her forehead and got up from the bed.

"I'll be right back."

She gritted her teeth and nodded, suddenly worried about handling the contractions on her own.

*****

A knock sounded, and Karen Martell looked up from her ironing to answer the door.

Adam Talbot was on her doorstep. Her heart beat a little faster at the sight of him.

"Mrs. Martell, Rachel is having the baby. Jason said to get you now."

"All right, come in. I'll get my bag and be with you in a minute. I have to get someone to stay with my children."

"I'll wait. I brought the buggy."

Karen walked into the dormitory from the room she and her children shared. She was the head of this building and therefore got a bedroom of her own.

"Daisy," she said to the young woman who sat in one of the rocking chairs in the parlor area of the dormitory. "Will you watch the children for me? Rachel is having her baby."

"Of course. Be sure and send word when the baby comes."

"I will. Thanks for watching the kids."

"Anytime."

Karen picked up her doctor bag and walked back to where Adam waited.

*****

After letting Karen off at the front door, Adam took the buggy to the barn.

Karen knocked and Michael Talbot, the middle brother, answered the door.

"Hi, Mrs. Martell, please come in. Rachel and Jason will be glad to know you're here."

"Thank you, Mr. Talbot. I'd like to see Rachel now."

"Certainly. This way."

"After all this time I know the way."

She walked up the stairs to Rachel and Jason's bedroom.

*****

Rachel closed her eyes and breathed a sigh of relief. "I'm so glad you're here. I think the baby is coming sooner than we thought."

Karen put her bag on the bureau and walked to the bed.

"Jason, will you excuse us, please? I'd like to check Rachel."

Karen scooped her hands in front of her and made moves as though pushing him out of the room.

Jason crossed his arms over his chest. "I'm staying. Rachel may need me."

"I'd like for him to stay." Rachel was afraid to have him leave. *What if I need him?*

"Very well, but stay out of my way, understand, and when I say do something, you do it. No questions."

"Understood."

Karen picked up her doctor's bag and brought it to the bed with her.

"Jason, do you have warm water and towels available? I need to wash my hands."

"Yes." Jason stood. "I brought up a bucket of hot water earlier. It should be just warm now. The bucket is on the floor by the commode."

"Good." She walked to the screen and called out. "Raise your knees and spread your legs, please. Let's see where you are in this process."

Rachel did as she was asked and flinched only a little at Karen's touch. Her belly was tender, and her bottom ached.

"Well, you're farther along than I thought you'd be. It looks like this little one is ready to come out. He's starting to crown." Karen straightened to address Rachel directly. "How long have you been in labor?"

"Since last night, but then they were only small pains, nothing big."

Karen set out her instruments on the bed. "Even small pains count as labor. With the big pains, we say you're in hard labor or the beginning of hard labor. Since the baby is crowning, I want you to push. Jason, if you want to stay, get yourself up by her head and let her hold your hands for support. Ready?" She paused. "Push. Again. Push with all your might."

Rachel pushed and bared down. She didn't feel like she could push any longer.

"All right. Rest a moment," said Karen.

After several sessions of pushing, Rachel didn't think she could do anymore and flopped against the pillows. "I'm so tired."

"I know, but you need to give me

another push. Just as hard as you can."

"Come on, love, you can do it." Jason stood beside the bed and Rachel's head. He held her hand, and she squeezed it as hard as she could when she was pushing.

She felt the support he gave her, appreciated that he would let her hold his hand and squeeze the heck out of it.

Gathering her strength, Rachel rolled her shoulders forward and pushed again with all her might and felt the baby move out of her body and then stop.

"Very good," said Karen. "The head is out, and he's got a full head of blond hair. Now give me a couple more just like that one and let's get him here."

Rachel did her best, and soon the baby slid from her body.

"Well," she asked, as she leaned on propped elbows. "What is it? Boy or girl?"

"I'll have to stop saying his and start saying hers. You have a beautiful baby girl. Let me get her cleaned up."

Soon, the sound of a slap followed by a small cry echoed through the room.

"She has quite a set of lungs, our little Abbie. You did so well. How are you, my love?" asked Jason, just before he leaned down and kissed her.

She gazed up at his grinning face. "She does, doesn't she? I'm tired and exhilarated and wonderful and can't wait to have her in my arms."

Jason helped her to sit up, fluffing the pillows behind her.

"Your wish is my command." Karen returned with the baby in a diaper and thin gown, swaddled loosely in a blanket.

Rachel held up her arms toward Karen. "Give her to me. Please. I need to hold her." She felt like a special connection had been broken.

Karen put the baby into Rachel's arms and stepped back.

Rachel laid the baby on her lap and unwrapped her. Together she and Jason counted her fingers and toes.

Abbie started to fuss.

"She doesn't like being messed with," said Rachel. "Maybe I should have left her wrapped."

Karen came back to the bed. "Jason, will you help her stand for a minute. I need to get the oilcloth off the bed and change the sheets. As soon as Rachel gets back in bed, Abbie will need to nurse."

Rachel stood, leaning against Jason for support while Karen quickly freshened the bed.

"There you go. All clean. Now, do you need help learning to feed her?"

Jason lifted Rachel and placed her back in bed.

"I don't know. Let's try and see." Rachel raised the baby to her breast and encouraged her to take the nipple by pinching her breast and putting the nipple near the baby's mouth. Soon the baby latched on, and all was well.

Karen packed up her bag. "Do you want me to tell everyone to come up? Better yet, I'll tell them Jason'll be down when you're ready for company."

Jason nodded. "I'll be down after Abbie is through eating."

"Very good." Karen grabbed her doctor's bag. "Now you stay in bed for a few days and drink lots of fluids and eat well. You're eating for two now. I'll be back tomorrow, to see how things are going and if you have any questions after tending her for a day. I know my way out."

"Thank you, Karen." Rachel looked up from the baby to utter the words and then went back to smoothing her hand over the baby's head. Her hair was so soft. It dried quickly and was soft as down. It was the softest thing she'd ever felt.

Jason sat back on the bed and ran his hand over Abbie's pale blonde hair.

Her head disappeared into her daddy's large hand.

"She's beautiful. Thank you." He leaned down and kissed Rachel slowly.

For a minute Rachel felt only the baby nursing and her husband's love. Soon Abbie let them know she was done with a little cry.

Rachel put the baby up on her shoulder and burped her.

"You can let the brothers know and invite them to meet their niece, after Billy. Have him come up alone first. He needs to meet his sister and for us to be a family."

Jason kissed her. "You're a good mother. I'll get him."

A few minutes later, Billy stood by the bed and stared, awe widening his eyes as he looked at the baby.

"She's so small."

"She is," said Rachel with a smile. "Would you like to hold her?"

His head snapped up, and he gazed at

Rachel.

"She's so little. What if I drop her?"

"You won't. Come around and get on the bed next to me and I'll set Abbie on your lap."

He grinned and nodded, then ran around the bed and crawled up beside his mother.

Rachel placed Abbie on Billy's lap and opened her blanket, so her arms were free.

Billy reached down and touched the baby's hand.

Abbie wrapped her fingers around his.

He looked up at Rachel, grinning.

"She likes me,"

"Yes, she does. Are you ready to be a big brother?" Rachel watched his face for his reaction.

Billy nodded. "Yup, and I'm gonna teach her everything she needs to know about Seattle. She'll know the best places to fish and I'll even show her my secret place. Not even Dad knows where that is."

Alarm shot through Rachel. "You should at least let your dad know where that is. If something happened to you we wouldn't know where to look. I don't want you to show your sister someplace where no one could find her. Understand?"

"Yes, ma'am. I guess that makes sense."

He looked at his father.

"Next time we go fishin' I'll show you my secret place."

Jason reached over and ruffled Billy's hair.

"I'd like that very much, son."

"Billy, why don't you get your uncles so they can meet their new niece."

"Okay."

He ran from the room.

"He'll be a good big brother." Jason slid in and took Billy's place next to Rachel.

"Yes, he will be. I'm so very happy." She looked down at Abbie then back at Jason. "Thank you for your wild scheme to bring one hundred women to Seattle."

"It worked out pretty well for us didn't it?"

"Yes, and for several of the other brides, too. Have I told you lately that I love you?"

"You haven't."

"I've been remiss in my duties." She stretched and kissed his waiting lips.

"You haven't been remiss. You gave me the greatest gift of love you can give. Our daughter. I love you."

She gazed down at their daughter

warmth filling her.. To her way of thinking, Abby was the most beautiful child ever. Rachel turned and looked at Jason, her husband, her one true love, and knew she was the luckiest woman in the world.

CYNTHIA WOOLF

ABOUT THE AUTHOR

Cynthia Woolf is the award winning and best-selling author of thirty-two historical western romance books and two short stories with more books on the way.

Cynthia loves writing and reading romance. Her first western romance Tame A Wild Heart, was inspired by the story her mother told her of meeting Cynthia's father on a ranch in Creede, Colorado. Although Tame A Wild Heart takes place in Creede that is the only similarity between the stories. Her father was a cowboy not a bounty hunter and her mother was a nursemaid (called a nanny now) not the ranch owner. The ranch they met on is still there as part of the open space in Mineral County in southwestern Colorado.

Writing as CA Woolf she has six scifi, space opera romance titles. She calls them westerns in space.

Cynthia credits her wonderfully supportive husband Jim and her great critique partners for saving her sanity and allowing her to explore her creativity.

TITLES AVAILABLE

MAIL ORDER MYSTERY – Brides of Seattle, Book 1

THE DANCING BRIDE - Central City Brides, Book 1
THE SAPPHIRE BRIDE - Central City Brides, Book 2
THE IRISH BRIDE - Central City Brides, Book 3
THE PRETENDER BRIDE - Central City Brides, Book 4

GENEVIEVE: Bride of Nevada, American Mail-Order
Brides Series, Book 36

THE HUNTER BRIDE – Hope's Crossing, Book 1
THE REPLACEMENT BRIDE – Hope's Crossing,
Book 2
THE STOLEN BRIDE – Hope's Crossing, Book 3
THE UNEXPECTED BRIDE – Hope's Crossing,
Book 4

GIDEON – The Surprise Brides

MAIL ORDER OUTLAW – The Brides of Tombstone,
Book 1
MAIL ORDER DOCTOR – The Brides of Tombstone,
Book 2
MAIL ORDER BARON – The Brides of Tombstone,
Book 3

NELLIE – The Brides of San Francisco 1
ANNIE – The Brides of San Francisco 2
CORA – The Brides of San Francisco 3
SOPHIA – The Brides of San Francisco 4
AMELIA – The Brides of San Francisco 5

JAKE (Book 1, Destiny in Deadwood series)
LIAM (Book 2, Destiny in Deadwood series)

ZACH (Book 3, Destiny in Deadwood series)

CAPITAL BRIDE (Book 1, Matchmaker & Co. series)
HEIRESS BRIDE (Book 2, Matchmaker & Co. series)
FIERY BRIDE (Book 3, Matchmaker & Co. series)
COLORADO BRIDE (Book 4, Matchmaker & Co. series)

TAME A WILD HEART (Book 1, Tame series)
TAME A WILD WIND (Book 2, Tame series)
TAME A WILD BRIDE (Book 3, Tame series)
TAME A HONEYMOON HEART (novella, Tame series)

THORPE'S MAIL-ORDER BRIDE, Montana Sky Series (Kindle Worlds)
KISSED BY A STRANGER, Montana Sky Series (Kindle Worlds)
A FAMILY FOR CHRISTMAS, Montana Sky Series (Kindle Worlds)

WEBSITE – http://cynthiawoolf.com/

NEWSLETTER - http://bit.ly/1qBWhFQ

CYNTHIA WOOLF

Made in the USA
Monee, IL
22 May 2023

34291956R00164